HEDGE KING IN WINTER

Christie,

Thanks so much for
your encouragement and
your own fantastic book.

Keep Writing!

Cover Illustration by Grafit Studios.
Cover and Interior Design by Glen M. Edelstein.
Map Design by Cornelia Yoder.

Dellert, Michael E. 1970–
        Hedge king in winter / Michael E. Dellert
        p. cm.
        ISBN 978-1-944400-00-2
        1. Fantasy. 2. Heroic Fantasy. I. Title.

Printed in the United States of America
First Edition: January 2016
1 2 3 4 5 6 7 8 9 10

To family, friends, and faithful companions all:
I wish you health, I wish you well, and happiness galore.
I wish you luck for you and friends; what could I wish you more?
May your joys be as deep as the oceans, your troubles as light as its foam.
And may you find sweet peace of mind, where ever you may roam.

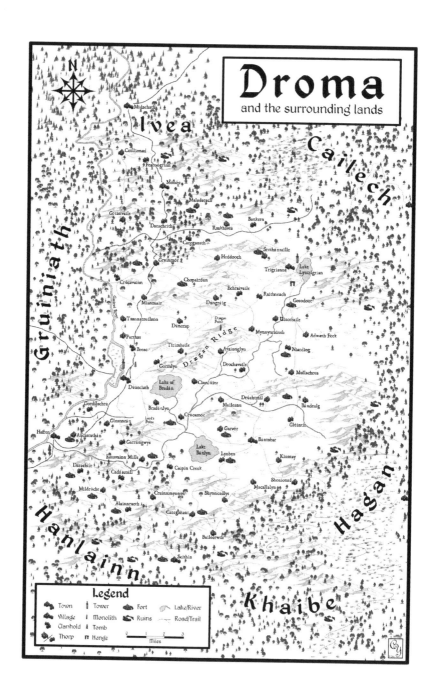

MAP OF DROMA AND THE SURROUNDING LANDS

PART ⊕NE

"DON'T 'COUSIN' ME, EOWAIN." Tnúthgal stood in the hall of the fort of Dúnsciath. He had five armed men at his back, and all of them had just come in from the road. Behind them, a flutter of terrified servants gawked from the courtyard of the fort as Tnúthgal shouted for the king in his own hall. "King Lórcan! Your people demand to see you! Where are you?"

Eowain stood, broad-shouldered and bearish, with his arms crossed over his chest. He had a plain, unadorned short sword at his belt. "Quiet down, Cousin. I'm telling you, he needs rest, that's all." Eowain lowered his arms and stepped forward.

King Lórcan, had been nine days in his sick-bed, wounded in an attempt to apprehend a criminal. His brother, the Lord Eowain had kept the kingdom running, but the king's condition was uncertain. Few beyond his circle of councilors even knew the exact nature of his injuries, and after nine days cloistered in his tower, the whole kingdom had become concerned for the king's life.

Eowain eyed his cousin up and down. Eowain wasn't a tall man, but nor was Tnúthgal. His cousin was grizzle-bearded with age, but no less burly than himself. Eowain knew him for a veteran of a fierce history, of a generation with his own father. As Eowain stepped forward, Tnúthgal did not shirk from him, bridling in his coat of steel-ringed leather.

The Lord-Drymyn Medyr walked into the hall and went nose-to-nose with Lord Tnúthgal, waving a finger in the old lord's face.

"The king has been wounded and he is being tended. On my authority, he's not to be disturbed until he is well enough to take back the helm of government. In the meantime, the Lady Rathtyen, Lord Eowain, and the King's officers are carrying on the business of the court. No doubt, the king will be well enough to see you before long. I will be sure he knows you called to convey your concerns."

"Lord-Drymyn Medyr." Lord Tnúthgal bowed, but his tone mocked. "I trust you are well."

"Do you now? I doubt that. But the king's not taking visitors, so unless you have some business before the court, out with you. And take your truncheon-wielding thugs with you. Go on. Out."

The five men bristled behind Lord Tnúthgal but he raised his hand to allay them. "You're lucky you're a drymyn, little man."

"Out." Eowain felt his brow twitch. The Lord-Drymyn had a seldom-heard edge in his voice.

The eyes of Tnúthgal's men widened. No doubt they feared the Lord-Drymyn's curse on them. But Tnúthgal only sneered. With disdain for the courtesies, he and his men went from the hall in a flurry of winter cloaks and ringing mail.

Medyr scolded the servants back to their duties. "Go on, then, all of you."

As the gathered household whispered away like diligent mice, Eowain took the Lord-Drymyn's shoulder and led him to the northern hearth, over which was mounted the mighty crest of a great elk. A trophy won by his father, who had once been king, as Eowain's brother now was king.

"Medyr?" The Lord-Drymyn was a scholarly man of some thirty summers, his red beard only lately mottled with grey. But Eowain felt how deceptively strong his arm was beneath his priestly robes, and knew the drymyn was allowing himself to be led. And Eowain had learned well from Medyr as a young man. The Gods despised those that harmed their servants, all the sacred tales said so.

But Eowain himself grew terse as they came away from the casual hearing of others. "Medyr, we can't keep lying to people."

"We're not lying. He's alive, he's recuperating, and we have the government well in hand until he recovers."

"I don't understand you. He's crippled. He can't be king of Droma. It's in the by-laws." Eowain felt piquant then.

Medyr nodded, nothing more. "I also know we need someone of Findtan's blood on the throne now. The *coelbreni* have told me so."

"As have I." Eowain's aunt, Lady Rathtyen, emerged from the kitchen. Eowain had left her aloft in the tower with his brother in order to attend to Tnúthgal. She was carrying her hands cupped together in front of her. She dashed a dozen wooden tiles inscribed with signs across the drinking-board of the hall.

Eowain felt his throat clutch with fear. They were each carved with a letter from the ancient language of the drymyn, and only those trained in their mysteries could fathom them. "Aunt—."

"Phoo!" She waved a hand at him and leaned over the tiles like an accounting clerk. "The trade relations of this tribe, the survival of these people, depend on my late husband's trade caravans and river-barges away down the Gasirad River. Farming and cattle are all well and good when they feed everyone. But when they don't, we need trade to beg, borrow, and barter for what we need with other tribes that have it. We can't do that without roads, caravans, barges, boat-docks and a proper market-place. And we can't finance those without the surplus we make from the king's estate. And the Gods won't favor the king's estate if he's crippled—." She stabbed at a constellation of tiles on the table.

Eowain was already worried enough, and the taut look on his mentor's sober features did nothing to reassure him. "The *coelbreni* say that a terrible winter will follow if Tnúthgal should become king. Many will die."

Rathtyen nodded at him. "Droma needs a king now more than ever. Lórcan has to abdicate, we all know it. But that doesn't mean we have to give up on the great work your father started here. Tnúthgal and Ninnid would have us neglect the wealth of ideas and innovations that trade brings with it. They'd have us digging our heads into the dirt, coaxing up crops and cattle. And sooner or later, the foreigners would overrun us, as we overran those before us. No, lad. I have friends who believe as we do, and we can turn to them now and secure their support."

Eowain felt indignation rising in his face. What were they telling him? "That's what Tnúthgal and the others were complaining about. They say Lórcan was only elected to the throne because your traders made it possible while the farmers in the uplands struggled."

"And who are 'they?' 'They' say a lot of things." Rathtyen waved away such arguments as if they were irrelevant. She took her nephew around the shoulder. "Listen here, my lad. You're right, your brother can't be king anymore. Tnúthgal and Ninnid will never stand for it, and they could raise a serious challenge if they worked together. We need to act fast—."

"The people have a right to select their king. It's an ancient right." Eowain looked back and forth between them until his gaze settled on his mentor. "Isn't that what you taught me?"

"Aye, lad. But sometimes the people can't be trusted to know everything that's at stake." He despaired with a shrug. "The portents are advantageous for your kingship, Lord Eowain. More so than for any of your cousins. You would have the support of the drymyn brotherhood. And your brother yet lives. That should work to our advantage maintaining the loyalty of the King's Company."

"I'm the captain of those men. They are loyal to Lórcan, I know it."

"More so than to their own families? Can you be sure?" Rathtyen shook her head. "Elections will break down into family factions. Families loyal to us, and those loyal to Tnúthgal. You can't tell me your men don't have families." She put her hand on Eowain's shoulder. "Stop fighting it, lad. You were a good son to your father, and you learned far more from him than you think. You have his fighting spirit, his honor, his love of the land and the people. You're disciplined, you're fair, and you're just. Your father would be proud." She arched an eyebrow at him. "There's just one thing you're not." His old widowed aunt turned to the Lord-Drymyn.

Medyr nodded his head to her and looked at him. "Married, my lord. You haven't got a wife, sir."

PART TWO⊕

LADY RATHTYEN RAISED her finger up into the air. "But don't you worry, we've already found a solution to that problem, haven't we, Medyr?"

Eowain hadn't been worried about it until then. "What? Married? Me?"

Medyr bowed. "Aye, if it please you, Lord Eowain, I've had word this morning from the fort at Trígrianna. The entourage of the Lady Fidelm of Dolgallu just passed through from beyond our borders, destined here in Dúnsciath in a few days." He nodded again and crossed his arms across his chest. "She is... a cousin to Ardghal, the king of Ivearda. Now wait! He seeks peace from the old feud between your family and his! You have a mutual enemy in the troublesome Cailech tribe between Ivearda and Droma." Medyr rocked back on his heels, nonchalant. "She is coming to negotiate terms for the marriage of her niece to our handsome king." And he bowed to Eowain again.

Rathtyen tapped Eowain on the forehead. "You have to think quick in times like these, lad. Why do you think dear cousin Tnúthgal is here with his thugs? He suspects Lórcan is dead or crippled and that we're hiding him to buy time."

Eowain gasped at her in disbelief. "Aren't we?" Weren't they? Hiding a crippled king to delay his abdication and the tribal vote for a new king? It was illegal.

Rathtyen blinked at him, bird-like. Dressed in widow's robes of black, Eowain thought once more how much she reminded him of an old raven. "Well of course we are, dear." Then she waved at the *coelbreni* tiles on the table. "That's not my point. My point is that he only thinks so because we've dallied over this for nine days."

Medyr made a grunt of agreement. "We had to contact—."

She put her hand up to Medyr. "We shouldn't have given him so much time to think." She closed her hand except for her upright thumb. "Tnúthgal is strong on the battle-field and popular among many of the cattle-chiefs." Then she put up her other fingers. "And it's been nine — count them, Lord-Drymyn, *nine* — days." Then she closed her other fingers save for one. "And now Tnúthgal wonders what we're up to here." She gestured to Medyr. "But—! Thanks to the good offices of our Lord-Drymyn here, we've got marriage prospects for you, though they come too late to be of much good to us."

• • •

THE FOLLOWING DAY, the King's forester came to the king's councilors with the strangest tale.

They were seated together in the king's office. Eowain was in his brother's place at the King's stout wooden desk. Wooden cubicles on the wall sheltered the detritus of a whole tribe's administration, scraps and scrolls of parchment scratched with ink. His four fellow ministers were comfortably seated across the desk. The stone walls of the tower made for close quarters, but it was customary for them to meet once a week in private with the king to share reports from the kingdom.

Beyond in the next room, King Lórcan lay in his bed, tended by his wife, his children, and the village chirurgeon. The last time Eowain had seen him, he was still sweating and feverish, delirious with pain and fever.

The forester was standing at his place. Aed by name, he managed and oversaw the uses to which the tribe put its woodlands. He was new in his job, the previous forest-warden having just crippled the King a mere ten days earlier, but he'd been a patrol lieutenant for time out of mind and Eowain had felt confidant assigning him the job until things could get sorted out.

Aed told how just the last night, he'd been out with his men on a patrol of the outlying farms, getting a better lay of the land. "The bandits, they was mounted on twelve light horses, my lord, and wore cheap boiled-leather cuirass for armor. Some bore shields and spears. But the rest, they had crossbows, like we seen the foreigners using lately, when they raided upriver in the spring. And these fellows was fighting openly with the village folk right in their very own fields."

There was a murmur among the King's Council. Eowain was the captain of the King's Company. He knew the crossbow was an expensive weapon to make, and not popular in his part of the creation. To see it in the hands of bandits on Droma's northeastern borders was worrisome.

"Go on." Eowain gestured for Aed to continue.

"Well, my lord, we charged in, me and my men. There was women and children down there fighting, we couldn't let that stand. They must've been giving the bandits the worst of it, though. The robbers saw us and rabbited for the woods. We left a few men for the wounded and chased them bandits into the wild beyond our fields."

Around the table, there were some encouraging nods. Eowain thought it sounded very brave to him, charging off into the wild like that after bandits. He missed those days. He'd been cooped up in court too long lately. Cooped up with his sick brother and his fellow ministers. Winter frost rimed the sealed wooden shutters, and felons were abroad. He should be leading a team to teach them how strong and proud the Donnghaile clan was. Instead, he was concerned about Medyr and Rathtyen's suggestions about abdication, coronation, and marriage.

But Aed went on. "We pursued them as far as we could see

them, but after a while, we lost them. That's where we found the old shrine."

Medyr's head rose from its study of the council table. "Old shrine? What old shrine?"

"There were signs to Echraide, the goddess of our tribe, my Lord-Drymyn. But there was much graffiti as well. Several of the holy signs had been defaced. And that's where we found the body." Aed the Woodward took a deep breath.

Eowain nodded. "It's alright, Aed. We all understand. Just tell us what you found."

Aed nodded and swallowed. "It was a body, my lords. A man's body, wrapped in dark robes. It was that trader, Marha."

Eowain remembered him. A prominent merchant known for being honest and good-natured, he'd been one of Lórcan's sturdiest supporters. And he'd disappeared a few weeks earlier.

"His skin was tattooed with symbols. The signs of some evil spirit, I've no doubt." Aed was an older man, a trapper and hunter all of his life. He squinted at the Lord-Drymyn, minister of all things spiritual in the kingdom.

"And where was this, Aed?" Eowain wanted to have it repeated for everyone around the office.

"Out to Bankern, my lord. On the northern border between the tribes of Ivea and Cailech."

Eowain nodded. "Thank you, Aed. Please, have a seat, and thank you for the bravery you displayed in chasing those bandits off."

"Aye, yer welcome, Lord." The old woodsman took his seat, rubbing his hands together. Eowain thought the scene must have disturbed the king's new forester very much.

The Lady Rathtyen was the first to speak. "Tnúthgal was just here with five of his own thugs yesterday. Now Bankern is threatened by bandits? The chief at Bankern is known to support Lórcan. It might be intimidation?"

"Bankern is a long way from Tnúthgal's estate." The chamberlain, master of the king's offices, sniffed and turned her nose up.

She had her dry brown hair bound up in a bun with a stick at the back of her head. "Why shouldn't they just be the usual Cailech scum haunting that no man's land between us and Ivearda?"

Eowain shook his head. "No. Crossbows aren't in the Cailech's arsenal any more than our own. They're foreigner weapons from downriver. Whoever is leading them is better-supplied than the typical Cailech rabble."

The chamberlain shrugged. There was no shortage of suspects. "Then why not the Ivea? They've never turned down a chance at a cattle-raid or a border-skirmish."

Medyr shook his head. "They were all mounted? That's unusual."

Eowain looked at the Lord-Drymyn. Yes, of course, he thought.

Medyr went on. "Who are bandits? Dispossessed farmers, exiles, orphans, tinkers, and ne'er-do-wells?"

Everyone about the table seemed to agree.

He shrugged and spread his hands wide. "So where'd they come into so many horses?"

Eowain could see Medyr's point. "Masterless soldiers."

Medyr leaned back, lighting a clay pipe with short puffs of smoke. "Bands of brigands desperate for hire and plunder. Their number has been growing since the King of Aileach took back his throne. They are legion, and they are hungry."

●   ●   ●

REPORTS ARRIVED THE NEXT MORNING. The Lady Fidelm's progress across Droma was nearing Dúnsciath. Eowain summoned Medyr and a patrol of cavalry-men to assemble.

He led the patrol out at the trot, leading them up the King's Trail east, into the hills away from the river. The news of bandits had troubled him, and no matter what came of this nonsense about marriage, he wasn't going to let a visiting king's noble kinswoman come to harm.

Eowain rode as one of his men, on a medium-sized hill-bred horse, and wore a gleaming shirt of ring mail over leather. He bore a wooden shield on his left arm, and held a spear tall and brilliant in the sun. At his belt, he wore a plain serviceman's short steel sword.

The hills along this stretch of the river were grassy and the soil rich, good pastureland in summer for horses and cattle. But this was winter. A rime of old snow and hoarfrost coated the ground. Brittle brown stubble was all that remained of the summer-grass. There against a hillside, a herd of milk-cows huddled for warmth in a byre. Mist rose from that congregation of kine and fell east toward the river, snaking through the hills.

Eowain thundered along with Medyr and his patrol behind him. He hadn't led them more than an hour along the trail before he met another of his scouts. "My lord! There's a scouting party of bandits within striking range of the Lady's progress."

Eowain shouted orders and spurred off down the trail. Medyr and the ten surprised horsemen spurred their own startled mounts to keep up with him.

Rounding the next bend, Eowain came in sight of the Lady Fidelm's entourage.

PART THREE

There had to be nigh on a hundred men-at-arms with her, some mounted and more a-foot, surrounding the carriage and wagons of this kinswoman of the King of Ivearda. *She's certainly making no attempt to hide her progress*, thought Eowain.

Some of the soldiers were in the gold, green, and white livery of Eowain's own clan, bearing the sigil of the river salmon. These were members of the King's Company dispatched from Trígrianna to escort the Lady Fidelm on her progress. But the blue, red, green, and gold livery, those were the men of her own Gwynn clan, and yet more numerous than his.

Away to the left, Eowain spied a dark knot of villainy fleeing away across the hills. *The bandit scouts*! Rancor rose in his throat. It shamed him that they had penetrated so far into the heart of the land, despite his best efforts. With a sharp cry, he spurred his steed and led his horsemen into a wild gallop.

The countryside rolled and rose north toward the far distant mountains, and the footing in the old snow and hoarfrost was insecure for the horses. Before long, Eowain cursed and drew up short. The villains had the advantage of a safe lead and had disappeared into the folds of the hills. He couldn't afford to risk valuable horses on a wild chase or an ambush.

Behind him, the lady's entourage had ground to a halt on the trail. Medyr, who had remained with the foot soldiers, rode out on his pony as Eowain returned from the brief chase. Eowain shook his head at the expectant look on the drymyn's face. "Cowards, that's what they were. Didn't get us a clear look at them. They could be from anywhere."

From the carriage emerged a tall, broad-shouldered, strong-looking woman with long flaxen hair. She was dressed in studded leather cuirass and carrying a sword at her belt, as if expecting battle. Two hard-eyed men took up positions at her shoulders as she proceeded across the field.

Eowain recognized her immediately, dismounted and knelt. "My Lady Fidelm, I am Eowain son of Findtan of Dúnsciath."

"Rise, my lord. It is a pleasure to see you again." She smiled at him and took him in an embrace.

"And you as well, my lady. It's been many years." He returned the smile. He'd spent a summer at the King of Ivearda's court as an honored guest. Or a hostage, depending on how one looked at such things. His father and the King of Ivearda had been unsuccessfully negotiating an alliance against Murdach King of Aileach. Eowain had been the surety for his father's good intentions. Eowain remembered the Lady Fidelm for her kindness to him when he was young, frightened, and far from home. He thought she looked remarkable for a woman of middle-ages, healthy and vigorous. *She's no house-marm, that's for sure.* He wondered for a moment what her niece must be like.

• • •

THE LADY FIDELM'S PROGRESS was a cumbersome affair. The mule-drawn wagons on the rough trails of the north Drægan hills were slow, and the spoked wooden wheels prone to breakage. The trails were rutted and littered with rough stones. What took a mere hour for Eowain and his horseman to travel that morning took two more days to return back to Dúnsciath with the Lady Fidelm's entourage. Eowain could see work needed doing come the spring to keep the roads open and passable.

Although she seemed friendly enough, Lady Fidelm insisted on remaining in her carriage. Eowain feared that didn't bode well for him. He wanted to speak with her, to make her understand what nonsense this whole notion of a marriage really was. He wouldn't become king, and a marriage between himself and a cousin of the Gwynn clan wouldn't end the feud if he wasn't going to be king.

Even if his brother did abdicate, there would be an election. One of his cousins, Tnúthgal or Ninnid, would be elected. They were much older than him, and more experienced in warfare and government. Eowain was sure he wouldn't be elected, no matter what Medyr and Rathtyen said. Lady Fidelm would be better off negotiating a marriage with one of his cousins. *Not that it would do any good.* The feud between the Gwynn and the Donnghaile went back nearly twenty years to the death of Asa of the Donnghaile as he returned from one of the wars with Hagall, murdered by a group of rebel Gwynn called the Wild Dogs. Asa had been close kin to Tnúthgal and Ninnid, and that blood was still bitter to them.

On the second morning of the journey back to Dúnsciath, Eowain received a report from his scouts. There'd been another skirmish between farm-holders and bandits, but this time in the southeastern forests. Many farmers' and foresters' lives were lost.

Medyr only nodded. "Your other cousin, Ninnid, away south in Scíthin."

Eowain gritted his teeth at the news. "So he's hiring thugs too now? Promising them plunder?"

"I would think so." Medyr shook his head. "If his thugs start growing overbold, we're going to have threats on two fronts before long. Tnúthgal and Ninnid might hate each other less than they hate you and your brother. If they do, we'll have trouble."

Eowain didn't have to guess at what he meant. If their cousins allied with each other against Lórcan, there would be more killing unless Lórcan abdicated and called for an election to replace him.

Or until Lórcan put down their rebellion himself. If Lórcan chose to stand and fight for his seat on the throne, Eowain as his brother and captain of his King's Company would have to lead that battle. The thought made his gut roil and his neck stiff. He rolled his helmeted head as he rode. Vertebrae crackled.

As the progress approached Dúnsciath, Eowain lead his men through the narrow defile where the Drægan ridge snaked down into the Gasirad river valley.

Villains in furs and leather rose from the dead winter grasses atop the hills to either side of the trail. Arrows pelted the Lady Fidelm's wagon, shafts quivered from its walls, and men cried out and went down from their horses with a crash.

Ambush! Eowain cried out, "To me!" and a lance of his horsemen chased off after him up the hillside. He crouched down in his saddle, bringing shield and spear to bear, feeling the blood pulsing in his temple as he spurred his mount.

And he cursed when once again he saw the bandits swinging up into saddles and fleeing on horseback into the north hills.

Damn it! Once again there was too much chance of losing footing in the snow, or being led into ambush. After only a brief pursuit, Eowain snarled with frustration, reined in and turned back with his men.

Medyr and Lady Fidelm were waiting for him with worried expressions. He looked over the procession, but they had things well in hand. Less than a handful of flesh-wounds, already bound and back in their boots and saddles.

Medyr shook his head and frowned. "That was too close to home."

"They can be anywhere," Eowain agreed. "We have to be everywhere." Bankern had been attacked two days earlier. There were raids in the South Wood. And now the Lady Fidelm's progress had been attacked not once, but twice.

Lady Fidelm's expression was stony. "Can't you and your brother keep order in your own house?"

Eowain rankled at the tone in her voice, but he couldn't very well argue with her. Dúnsciath, the king's seat, was twelve good miles from Bankern as the raven flew, but not so far from the forested hills that Tnúthgal controlled to the north. If the brigands had a base camp somewhere nearby, Tnúthgal should have known about it. And yet, Eowain hadn't heard anything about such a camp, nor had any of Tnúthgal's chiefs been raided.

Eowain could see the angle. If Tnúthgal took leadership of the tribe by force, he could replace Lórcan's loyal land-holders by promising plunder and lands to the bandits. Many people would die, many more would be wounded, and there would be disease, hunger, refugees, orphans, and widows. A generation of men might be lost if this escalated into a civil war.

But would Tnúthgal really risk a war over this? Surely, Tnúthgal must know Lórcan's wounds aren't so bad?

Eowain drummed his fist on the saddle before him and frowned at Medyr. "We need to get some intelligence on this. That was bold, even for our usual brigands. And no crossbows this time. Short bows."

Medyr nodded. "Poachers' weapons."

Eowain stroked at his beard. "So this gang is growing now." He ticked off his fingers. "Horses? Crossbows? Short bows?"

Lady Fidelm frowned at both of them. "And they have too many men by far. This is a dangerous game you're playing, my lords."

Eowain didn't want to admit she was right. Surely these bandits could be put down. Surely, any differences between Lórcan and Tnúthgal could be evened out.

The progress went on. The sun settled down in the west over the Gruiniath hills beyond the river. Eowain escorted the Lady's entourage down the trail from the uplands and into the camp ground set aside on Dúnsciath's southeast end for traders and visitors of all kinds. The king's tower stood proud on its rocky outcropping over the river.

Eowain was tired and his nerves had been rattled by the ambushes along the trail. He wanted very much to have these wedding negotiations done. It was all a waste of time, he was sure. Lórcan would not be forced to abdicate, elections would not be held, and everything would go on much as it had before. Without an unwed king to seal an alliance with the Gwynn, there was no point in even discussing the matter, he was sure.

But despite himself, he offered the Lady Fidelm a night's rest from her travels before meeting with the court of Lórcan. She graciously accepted. He could see in the lines of her face that she was weary. She'd come all the way from Ivearda in that carriage of hers, drawn by those painfully slow mules. No doubt, she looked forward to a restful night in the security of the camp.

Medyr excused himself to attend to matters at the shrine in the town, and Eowain went on up to the tower alone, tired and peckish. He was in want of fresh clothes, a hot meal and a good cup of *ôl*.

The news at the tower, however, was no less frustrating. Lórcan had been seen by the staff and soldiers of the fort, but only from the window of the tower. He hadn't gone out among the people. The King had waved from the window and raised a strong fist to the sky, but appeared heavily bandaged and soon retired. He'd remained in seclusion since, and the whole event had failed to assure the people of their King's well-being. Even Eowain's own request to see his brother was denied by the chirurgeon, who claimed the King was sleeping.

But there were no further reports of other bandit attacks, nor had any evidence emerged that linked the bandits to his cousins.

After a hot meal and a cup of *ôl*, Eowain went to bed, saddle-sore and muttering curses.

•   •   •

OVERLOOKING THE KING'S HALL in the manor of Dúnsciath was a large round window. Eowain was admiring the beauty of it. A showpiece of stained glass, his father, the late King Findtan, had had it imported from Naricia at no small expense. The morning sun was caught up there in the glass, twinkling in shades of white, green, gold, the family colors, on a field of blues and reds.

He'd been glad to see Lórcan back at the head of the King's table in the hall. Seated before all his councilors, his brother was wide-eyed, alert, and furious. But Eowain feared now that it was all in vain.

Lórcan pounded his good right fist on the board, drawing Eowain's attention down from the glass and back to the matters at hand. "I won't abdicate!" Lórcan cursed floridly. "Not if this is what's going to happen. We can't allow banditry and lawlessness to undermine everything father and I worked for."

Medyr stood up. "My king, you know of my love for you, your father, and all your good works. But our laws forbid a crippled man from being king. It's the king's duty to be the sacred husband to the land. For the land to be whole, its king must be whole. You risk bringing plague, famine, and war down on us. That's what the law says, and that's what Tnúthgal will say against you."

Lórcan waved impatiently at his white-robed drymyn. "I ought to know that nonsense well enough. You and Rathtyen poured it in my ear all through growing up. But I never slept with any 'goddess of the land,' I can tell you what. All I got was my wife. That's all Eowain's going to get too, a wife. I'm not going to abdicate just because some ancient law says so." He raised his left arm and shook it at all of them.

It was clear enough to Eowain now. Clear enough to everyone in the king's hall. He'd lost the two last fingers of his left hand.

But Lórcan didn't seem to care, shaking the hand as he went on. "*This* doesn't have to be the end of a kingship!"

Medyr shook his head, adopting the tone of a patient parent with a recalcitrant child. "In better and more sympathetic times, perhaps not, my lord. But Tnúthgal has already been here once to call you out in front of witnesses. We've seen three skirmishes with bandits in the last five days. Patrols have reported robbers skulking through the hills and forests. We need a king on the throne to rally the people against these disturbances. But the people won't rally to you, my lord. Not crippled as you now are." Medyr shrugged as if the matter was out of his hands. "I'm sorry, my lord. Your kingship has already ended. We just haven't announced it yet."

There was silence at the table. Rathtyen was uncommonly quiet. The king's chamberlain and forest warden seemed to find the floor and the walls immensely interesting. Even Eowain looked away, at the enormous rack of the Great Elk over the hearth.

He thought he knew what this must mean to Lórcan. Their father had raised him to be a king, the next king after himself. When Findtan died, Medyr had agreed with Rathtyen that it was important for the kingdom that Lórcan succeed their father. Without an election, they'd bribed and cajoled the kingdom's clients to make Lórcan's succession happen. But without Medyr's support now—?

Eowain looked at Lady Fidelm. The foreign noblewoman. Eowain had heard she was from some remote village far away in the mountains, a country-cousin to the King of Ivearda and not a resident at his court.

But court-wise or not, she seemed not the least bit uncomfortable in that silence. Fidelm stood and addressed the King. "Lórcan, you know I'd be happy to let you continue playing at being king. But your people are of no use to us if they're fighting among themselves. My people need security now from these bandits on our borders, just as yours do. I would see us unite our families, put this old feud to rest, and bring order back to the lawless lands between Ivearda and Droma." She waved a hand to Rathtyen and Medyr. "You will not be king here long, even if you are king now. It's clear your own people, your own drymyn even, won't support you. So an alliance with you alone is worthless to us. But if your brother is king? Then your family remains in control of great wealth and assets. And maybe your tribe remains united against threats like Ivea to your north, or the Cailech between us." She nodded to Eowain and Rathtyen. "I'm sure your family will find a proper place for you in their new regime."

Lórcan looked long and hard at her.

As his brother, Eowain wanted to defend him, to support him.

So he agreed with Lórcan. The loss of his king's left hand seemed not so bad. His right had always been the stronger hand anyway. He was still good for a fight, and there was nothing wrong with his mind, aside from bull-headed stubbornness.

But the law required an abdication, Medyr as drymyn had said so. By law, there would be an election, and surely Tnúthgal would be the next king. After all, who would elect Eowain, young as he was? And if Eowain wasn't willing to fight for his claim, then what?

But the bandits? Were they strong-arm tactics, thugs in their cousin's employ?

Eowain remembered a time his father Findtan had taken men across the river to negotiate with the bastard Gruin-men. He remembered he was maybe fourteen summers at the time. *Gods, was that really six years ago already?* He remembered it was a cold day in early spring. The sky was blue and the clouds were high, scudding across the sky in a stiff breeze. The Gruin-men, there were maybe twenty of them, and they were a ragged, dirty lot, but they were armed to the teeth behind one of their kings.

Eowain remembered his fear too well. And his father knew he was scared. While they waited on their hill for the heralds of each side to prepare the ground where the meeting would take place, Findtan took hold of Eowain's shoulder. "Don't be afraid," he said. "Look there." He pointed to the cousins. There were four of them, hard men, veterans of many battles. There were the brothers, Tnúthgal with his wicked-looking spear and Ninnid with a sword clutched in a fist. There was Sétnae whose grandfather was a holy-man, and there was Airnetach who had married well. All stood silent. None looked at the knot of Gruin-men in plain sight on the opposite hill. Instead they scanned the forested hills all about for the Gruin-men that could not be seen. Findtan had said to him then, "Trust your cousins against all the world."

But then he'd pointed to Lórcan, who stood in a chariot of his own, rings of steel on his jerkin glinting in the sun. And his brother's eyes had scanned not the gang of men ahead of them, nor the countryside all around. His brother's eyes were on their cousins. And Findtan said then, "But trust your brother against your cousins."

That had been his father's lesson to him, and to his brother. "Nothing counts so much as blood. The rest are just strangers."

So Tnúthgal and Ninnid were wrong if they planned to drive Lórcan from the throne with a gang of lawless resolutes. Eowain would see to it.

Eowain shook his head. *No.* He wouldn't roll over on his brother. "I do not want the kingship. And it would be wrong not to give the people an election. But it would be equally wrong to give the throne to Tnúthgal or Ninnid if they're going to put our own common people in harm's way for it. I say we don't announce your condition yet, but we appear together often here, and I appear in the countryside, leading things. When you're fit to be seen in the field again, we can cross the bridge of abdication or not."

Eowain imagined he saw gratitude in his brother's eye. He was sure he felt appreciation in the grip of his king on his shoulder.

Fidelm shook her head. "That is unacceptable to us. Our alliance with Droma is conditioned on Eowain being king. I don't believe Lórcan will hold the throne a whole moon before someone overthrows him. Please, Lórcan." She pleaded with him. "Your own drymyn admits that he can't protect you from the law. Your wise aunt and I are asking you to do this thing sooner rather than later. The Gwynn can support Eowain's claim, along with the Lady Rathtyen and the Order of the Drymyn, and offer my niece in marriage to make peace between our families. But if you insist on holding the throne, I cannot agree to any promise of marriage, and you will lose the Gwynn as a potential ally. We cannot ally ourselves with a cripple."

Lórcan looked long and hard at Eowain. Eowain stared back at him. They had played well together at hurling across the village pitch as young men. Eowain felt no animosity between them, knew there need be no shouting, indeed no speaking or signing of any kind, for him to know his brother's mind.

Eowain had to make a decision. For his brother's own pride.
For Father's memory. He stood up. "Lórcan is still the king until
he says otherwise. In the meantime, as his master of horse, I am
taking command of the King's Men for the duration of our emer-
gency. We will put Tnúthgal in his place first. And Lady, please
remain with us at court for a few days and enjoy our hospitality.
While you are here, I should like to discuss this alliance between
our families more fully. There are other ways our two tribes can
cooperate against the Caillech and move toward peace."

The lady seemed dissatisfied. "Eowain, why won't you argue for
your right to become king?"

Before Eowain could find words, Medyr spoke up. "He believes,
my lady, as we all do, in the traditional ways of our people. He
believes in ideas like truth, honor, and family."

She snorted at the drymyn. "So we're going to go on with this
ridiculous farce a while longer?" She slapped her hands on the table
and shook her head. "Gods and Shynn forgive me, Lórcan, but
better for your kingdom if you'd died that day. Then your brother
would have less of a damned choice."

PART FOUR

ANOTHER NIGHT AND DAY and night passed. Eowain met with the councilors of Lórcan and the Lady Fidelm to seek some agreement on the marriage contract.

Eowain was ambivalent on the subject. On the one hand, he knew it was his duty, his obligation to his family, that he find a suitable wife and sire children to carry on the name and line of Donnghal and Findtan. He did not take such obligations lightly.

But on the other hand, he'd been in love once before.

Aine of Gailenga was her name. She was a beautiful thing, cousin of the lord in Larriocht to whom he'd been fostered. Despite the fashion of the day, she wore her hair cropped short, and her neck was long, slender, supple as a swan's. He was not quite a man, not quite fourteen summers old. She was two or three years his senior. So graceful, so delicate, with an enchanting smile and a bewitching laugh.

He would have followed her around for hours like a puppy dog if he'd been allowed. He used to arrange the course of his days to take him where he thought he might see her. She and her friends were favorites among the young warriors that served his foster father. She and they went to every hurling match, cheering for the local heroes on the pitch.

One day, in a mad fit of foolish courage, he'd approached her at one of those games. He'd put his hand upon her shoulder and she'd turned to him. By the power of whatever madness possessed him, he asked then and there for her troth.

She was a sensible lass, more sensible than he by far. He was only a foster-son of her lord, not even a man yet, a boy of no name and no particular fortune, son of a minor hedge king from the back wood hills.

"No," she said. Like a spear, it struck him in the chest, that singular word. "No." As final as a doom.

He had never consider that she might reject him. Never thought she wouldn't love him.

But she did, and she didn't. And he'd made a terrible fool of himself. And she'd broken his heart.

Eowain had no great desire to repeat such an experience. Whatever agreement they came to regarding a marriage to this niece of the Lady Fidelm, the lass herself had the right to agree to the proposal, or to reject it. Eowain did not need to imagine how humiliating such a rejection might be.

And there was the matter of the kingship. The Lady Fidelm was stubborn on this point. Without the kingship, Eowain's rank at court meant little to her. If the kingship went to Tnúthgal or Ninnid or one of his other cousins, Eowain, as a son of Findtan, would be the youngest scion of the disenfranchised branch of the family. It might be ten or twenty years before the kingship might be available to him again, and he would have lost the advantage he currently held, as the captain of the King's Company and the king's brother. By such reckoning, he might never become king.

Of course, Eowain had never really expected to be king of Droma. His father was king, so he'd always known he had a claim, for sure, but the Donnghaile weren't a small clan. There were four cousins older and more experienced than he. After all, he was only twenty summers old. Sure, he'd been in the King's company for six years already, even worked his way up to captain when Lórcan became king. He'd seen his share of war and led his men into battles.

But to actually run the kingdom? Even Lórcan didn't know much about that when Father died in the field and he wasn't much older then than Eowain was now. And he probably wouldn't have succeeded, except that Murdach of Aileach had been wounded and overthrown. His usurper, our ally, had insisted on Lórcan winning the succession, and Medyr and Rathtyen had bribed and cajoled the chief-holders of the tribe to elect him.

But that alliance had proven ill-founded. It wasn't long before the usurper was overthrown in turn. Murdach sat again on the throne of Aileach. Eowain doubted very much that Murdach would want to see another son of Findtan, his betrayer, on the throne in Droma.

And so the negotiations with the Lady Fidelm dragged on, with no real progress being made.

• • •

ON THE FOLLOWING MORNING, the Lord Tnúthgal returned to the fort of Dúnsciath with his thugs. He sat a-horse in the king's own courtyard and called Lórcan to come down from his tower and face him.

Eowain went behind Lórcan with Medyr. His brother's hand and arm were bandaged and slung, bound close to his chest. It was unclear how many fingers he had, they were so baffled with bloody linens.

Lórcan, proud and arrogant, bore himself forth from the hall. As they marched across the lawn of the courtyard, Eowain cast glances to his lieutenant and such sergeants of the King's Company as he thought he could trust. They put aside whatever tasks they had in hand and rose to join their king. Behind them, more men from the rank and file fell in as well, until Eowain had a dozen men behind the king, compared to Tnúthgal's five.

Lórcan waved his good hand at their cousin. "Enough of this shouting in my courtyard. What would you have of me, cousin? To know I'm hale and healthy? I'm not, but I'm recovering a-pace. In the meantime, Eowain has taken command of the King's Company, and my staff are working under the direction of Rathtyen and Medyr."

"I'm glad to see you up and about, cousin. I'm sure I speak for the whole kingdom when I express my relief and my wishes for your health."

"Gracious wishes, I thank you, cousin. Do we have business to discuss, or did you call me down from my bed just to wish me a good day?"

Tnúthgal dismounted and removed his riding gloves, kneeling a moment in the dirt to serve courtesy. "We do have some small business, King Lórcan. Would it trouble you to sit and discuss it over a game of fickle?"

"A game of fickle, is it? Very well then. Come into the hall. We shall have a game."

• • •

LÓRCAN SETTLED INTO a large comfortable arm-chair, leaning back as servants set up the board between them. Tnúthgal took a seat on the enclosed bench designed to capture the warmth from one of the hearths. There were rugs and cushions strewn round-about on which the rest of Lórcan's court made themselves comfortable.

It was customarily expected that the leaders of Droma were more than just warriors or priests. To be complete, they had to also be well-versed in artistic skills. For the well-bred, contests in poetry, painting, or other arts were a popular and frequent event. Winners of these contests gained honor while losers risked humiliation and loss of favor. The outcome of such contests could greatly affect a person's standing in the kingdom.

The game of fickle was an ancient one, more than a thousand years old, a time-honored tradition famous in many a song and story. The name, "fickle," was very old and meant "wood sense," though no one alive knew why. It was said to have been invented by Trógain himself, the god of light and inspiration. It was said his son, Conderc, played skillfully at the game, and that legendary King Kynvawr spent a third of every day playing it.

Eowain took a seat near to the gaming table, the better to see how his brother was doing.

The drymyn Medyr settled nearby on a cushion with one of his acolytes beside him. Eowain's Aunt Rathtyen fluttered about until a chair was brought. She refused to sit upon the floor, cursing the servants for not considering the weakness in her loins and lower back.

The Lady Fidelm too made herself comfortable with her few ladies in attendance on her.

The servants finished their business and Eowain took a moment to see that all was in order. The board itself was in the shape of a circle. It was chequered, divided into seven concentric and quartered rings.

Medyr reached out a hand and pointed to the starting arrangement of nine pieces, four of black, four of white, and one, the King-Stone, of grey. He whispered to his acolyte. "The pattern of the board is symbolic, as is the fact that there is only one King piece whose natural place is at the center of the board."

"How so?" The acolyte leaned forward to look at the board, his brows furrowed.

Lórcan called for a pitcher of ôl and cups. "I have a powerful thirst." Eowain knew thirst was a consequence of the herbs that Medyr had given him for his pain. He worried now that the numbing effect of the herbs might expire before the game was finished. With experienced and evenly matched players like Lórcan and Tnúthgal, a game could last for several hours. What effect would the pain have on Lórcan's game?

Medyr went on explaining the game while the court waited for ôl. "The pattern of the fickle board presents to our eyes the lineaments of the cosmos as we perceive them." Medyr's hand mimicked the circles of the board, and the crossings of the lines upon it. "The pattern of seven concentric circles around the sacred Center mirrors the seven Wanderers of the Night in the skies above, circling about us here on Abred. The radial divisions of the quartered circle combine with the circles to represent the great Wheel of the Year. There is the line of the solstices, there the line of the equinoxes. At the four points of the compass are the Great Days of the Year."

Eowain stroked at his beard as he half-listened to Medyr. He and Lórcan had learned the game together at the drymyn's knee, he'd heard it before, many times. Fickle was a game of kings and drymyn. In the old tales, the heroes often proved their noble rank by showing they could play the game, and so the finer points of its rules and tactics were required learning for many a young nobleman.

Servants came with pitchers and cups for Lórcan and his court. Eowain took one and let the servant-girl pour it full. He knew Tnúthgal for an excellent player, so he imagined it would be a long game.

Medyr's lesson went on. "The twenty-four segments of the outer circle represent the hours of the day, and the waxing and waning of the moon in each month."

Eowain took a long draught of his *ól*. It was sweet with malt, but bitter with an herbal gruit of sweet gale, mugwort, yarrow, horehound, and heather that gave it the distinctive flavor for which the local brewers were known. He savored it on his tongue for a long moment.

Medyr continued, but Eowain remembered the lessons well enough. *The four quarters of the board represented the four great traditional kingdoms of Iathrann: Gruiniath, Hagall, Laigan, and Muvain.*

"That, basically, is how the pattern of the board evolved, a pattern equally able to represent time, space and many other dimensions of experience." Medyr paused to receive his own cup of ól and drink from it. "The board represents the King's realm, with the seat of power at the center. The contest is to take possession of the King's seat."

Eowain knew the game was supposed to reflect the larger divisions of Iathrann, the great provinces and the High-Kingship. The

land of Droma was one of the many tribal kingdoms that formed
the eastern province of Hagall, and Droma had sent many young
men to war, sometimes successful and sometimes not, to secure the
High-Kingship for Hagall. For now, the King of Gruiniath, over
the river to the west of Droma, was the High-King. But Eowain
had heard rumors that their own King of Hagall had ambitions.

"The beauty of the opening arrangement is that it neatly chimes
with the board's symbolism." Medyr pointed to the circle in the
middle of the board. "At the center sits the King-Stone in a small
province in the shape of a perfect quartered circle. Immediately
flanking it are four White pieces representing the provincial rulers
in their aspect of allegiance."

Eowain reflected on their present predicament. If Lórcan was
the king at the center, who were the four white stones representing his allies? The forest warden Aed? The chamberlain Neued?
Medyr? Himself?

He could repeat the rest of Medyr's fickle lesson from memory.
*The boundaries of the four great provinces are defined by the extended arms of the central
cross. Because it is on borders that disputes most often occur, Black pieces sit on their
extremities. Midway between these on the outer circle are White pieces standing for the
inner harmony of each province whatever their conflicts with each other.*

Certainly, there were disputes on Droma's borders, and
between neighbors within the kingdom. But Eowain remembered
the days when his father had ruled as king. Days when it had
seemed to Eowain that all men loved and respected one another.
But he was just a boy then. What had he known about the ways of
the world?

Medyr completed the lesson by pointing to the remaining black
pieces. "Finally at the center of each province sits a Black piece representing the provincial rulers in their aspect of rivalry with each
other and opposition to the center."

And what of the black stones, Lórcan's rivals? Eowain counted them off
in his thoughts. *Tnúthgal, certainly. Maybe our other cousins too?* Ninnid,
Setnae, and Airnetach all had as much claim to the throne as

Tnúthgal. If all four rose against Lórcan, how long would he hold the throne? *Not long,* Eowain reckoned.

Medyr smacked at his *ôl* and warmed to his subject. "Of course, fickle also reflects a more profound conflict, the eternal conflict between the cosmic principles of Order and Chaos. Order is forever trying to establish peace and harmony in the world. Chaos is forever trying to disrupt this. Or," said the drymyn, casting a weather eye on Tnúthgal, "the one is forever trying to stifle enterprise and adventure, while the other tries to liven things up a bit."

Tnúthgal gave Medyr a withering sidewise look, but Lórcan was now introducing the game. "We play by Cathá's Rules." Lórcan gestured at the lines radiating out from the center. "White's aim is to create a continuous (not necessarily straight) line of stones linking the King-Stone to the outer ring." He gestured to the four black stones around the circumference of the circle, and the four black stones seated at the center of each quarter. "Black's aim is to force White to resign, either by cutting off the center, or by reducing White's strength to less than seven stones."

Eowain heard the whisper from Medyr's acolyte. "Why less than seven stones?"

"It's the minimum number of stones necessary to create a line out from the center."

Lórcan seemed not to notice the lesson being given. "The first to succeed is the winner. Cousin, choose a side, Black or White?"

Tnúthgal inclined his head to Lórcan with a respect that hinted of mockery. "You are the King of Droma, Your Highness. You should be White."

That's good, thought Eowain. White started with an advantage. If Lórcan could make the most of it, he might win the game in the opening stage of the game. But if he didn't, the advantage would shift to Tnúthgal.

Eowain heard another whisper from Medyr. "Each side starts with eight stones on the board, as well as the King-Stone, which starts on the side of White. They then have another nineteen stones with which to win the game."

The colors were agreed, and so Lórcan moved first. They took turns placing a stone at a time into the vacant holes at the intersections between the rings and the lines on the board.

Eowain watched the game unfold. Lórcan and his white pawns had a definite advantage and made an initial attempt at a decisive victory. But Tnúthgal was an experienced player and Lórcan soon gave up this strategy.

All of Tnúthgal's black pawns were focused on blocking him. But while Tnúthgal was clever enough to prevent an outright win, his black pawns were kept on the run. Lórcan sought to establish several lines across the third, fourth, and fifth rings. These rings were the easiest for Tnúthgal to secure, but it was no easy thing for Tnúthgal to stop Lórcan from establishing strong lines across them. There were several standard moves to which Tnúthgal was no stranger, and he selected Morann's Gambit, grinding down Lórcan's advantage and forcing the game toward the second stage.

Pawns were captured by surrounding them on two sides with opposing stones, but Lórcan and Tnúthgal were careful not to engage in wholesale massacres in the early stages. Eowain had practiced with Lórcan often enough to know that this strategy could backfire. In the transition from the first stage to the second stage, the advantage turned to the side that still had pieces in hand to place on the board.

As the game progressed and a second pitcher of ól was passed around, Eowain began to worry. It didn't seem as if Lórcan was checking the safety of his pieces in the innermost ring.

"The contest is livened," explained Medyr to his acolyte, "by an ambivalence in the nature of the King-Stone. This reflects the reality that though the High King is the natural champion of Order, too much Order is no better than too much Chaos. Thus, in certain circumstances the King-Stone is liable to change sides."

The King-Stone was considered as White only until Black's pieces started to move on the board. Then it counted as either color for capturing stones in the inmost circle. Tnúthgal could use the King-Stone himself to secure the inner circle and force an abdication.

Eowain had many times forgotten this treacherous nature of the King-Stone. For the White player, such an oversight could be devastating.

Then a thought occurred to Eowain that he'd never had before. When his father and his brother had been named as King, they'd been brought to the sacred burial mound of their ancestors, upon which there was a sacred stone: the stone of Echraide, goddess of Droma. Lórcan and his father before him had to stand upon that stone in order to be named king. *Is the King-Stone not, then, the king himself, but instead the sacred stone upon which the king was crowned?*

It had been more than an hour since the game started and the first phase was only just coming to an end. All the twenty-seven pieces on each side had been placed. Many on each side had been captured. Tnúthgal had nearly succeeded in making the third and fourth circles impassable.

This would have been fatal for Lórcan in the second phase, but Tnúthgal had executed the move too early and so it proved to be merely an inconvenience. Lórcan was able to shift his offensive from one line to another.

But none of his lines through the middle rings were as strong and secure as they should have been. With both players' pieces moving on the board, the underlying advantage passed to Tnúthgal's black pawns. Eowain knew that in the absence of any bold plan, White's best bet was to consolidate avenues to the circumference and avoid losing pieces.

Tnúthgal was moving to blockade the center with an impenetrable wall. It was a cheap way to win, using the King-Stone to capture and secure the inmost circle. But Eowain knew it was an unlikely strategy. A barricade by Black was seldom more circular than White's lines were straight.

The game was dragging now into its third hour. The heat and the smoke from the hearth had grown stifling. Another pitcher of ól went around. Several members of the court excused themselves, while others arrived and settled down to watch the game in progress.

The inner and middle rings seemed reasonably secure, and Tnúthgal had set about capturing as many stones as possible. It was not uncommon by this stage of the game for some pattern to emerge, indicating the eventual winner.

Tnúthgal slammed his tankard on the table, rattling the board and pieces. He reached out, moved a black stone one space clockwise. "Challenge!" His shout was exultant.

Everyone leaned forward to examine the board.

"What? What's going on?" The acolyte seemed confused.

"Black's aim is to force White to resign, by either cutting off the center or reducing White's strength to less than seven pieces." Medyr pointed to the board. "Lord Tnúthgal believes that he has done so. By tradition, King Lórcan, once challenged, must either win outright or capture a Black stone within the next five moves."

Part Five

MORE OFTEN THAN NOT, no challenge was necessary for White to recognize defeat. Only in cases of stubbornness was the challenge typically invoked. Eowain had learned the hard way that one had to be very sure of oneself to issue a challenge, for the price of a failed challenge was often a victory for White.

But this had been a devious game. Even now, Eowain could see no clear winner. The southwest and southeast quadrants had been barricaded, as had the western line. The eastern and north-eastern corridors were being closed to Lórcan, with the only gap in that quarter being irrelevant. But Eowain could see weaknesses in Tnúthgal's north, northwest, and southern lines. He would have to close those gaps and prevent a capture of one of his own stones to win the game, for surely, Lórcan had more than enough White pawns on the board.

Now the room grew hushed. At the backs of the gathered court, the fire crackled and smoky pine-wood sizzled and popped, but the spectators of the king's game seemed to hold their collected breath.

Lórcan moved, and Tnúthgal quickly countered. No more waiting, Eowain could see that. Tnúthgal was certain of himself.

But Lórcan waited a long time, observing the board, sipping at his *ôl*. He rubbed at the bandages on his wounded hand. Were the herbs fading? Was Lórcan's mind plagued by pain? Would he be able to think through these next few moves? He reached out to the board and hesitated, hovering over one of his stones for a moment. Then he committed himself.

Tnúthgal grunted with satisfaction, moved a stone, and another of Lórcan's pieces was captured. The strength of the White stones had dwindled dangerously.

Eowain could see the strain on his brother's face now. As Lórcan rubbed again at the bandages on his left hand, it was certain that the effects of the herbs had subsided. But the king said nothing. He examined the board, seeking a way out of the encirclement. Even if Tnúthgal's victory wasn't entirely certain, Lórcan had to fight his way to the outer circle or capture one of Tnúthgal's pieces in the next three moves, or else surrender.

Abruptly, Lórcan reached out and moved a piece. It looked like he'd take one of Tnúthgal's pieces on the next move. But Tnúthgal saw it too and moved another piece. Lórcan cursed as another of his White pawns was taken.

The assembled courtiers gasped. Eowain grimaced. It had been a foolish move, he could see that, and Lórcan had wasted an opportunity and lost yet another of his pawns. He still had more than enough pieces to break out to the edge and win the game, but he was running out of opportunities to do so. And if he lost to their cousin in his own hall, whilst he was wounded? Eowain feared for his brother's reputation.

"Brother—?" But Medyr put a restraining hand on Eowain's arm and shook his head. It wouldn't be right for him to speak up. His brother had to win or lose on his own. Eowain ground his teeth together and held his tongue.

Lórcan rubbed once more at his bandaged hand. Tnúthgal smirked as he feigned concern. "Are your wounds troubling you, Your Highness?" Eowain felt a rising anger and clenched his jaw.

Lórcan shrugged. "A small matter." But Eowain could see the color had drained from his brother's face, leaving him pale and clammy. The game had drawn on for nearly three hours already.

"Do you remember the song of King Nudd, Your Highness?"

Tnúthgal's question was unexpected, but Eowain knew the tale. King Nudd had been a king in ancient times, before Men came to these lands. He'd been crippled in a great battle with evil monsters, and forced to abdicate the throne to his treacherous kinsman, Bres.

Lórcan grunted. "I'm sure I don't." Eowain knew he did. Any small child knew that tale.

"Lost his hand to the Avacna in battle?"

Lórcan leaned forward to study the board. "Doesn't ring a bell."

"His kinsman Bres had to become king?"

Eowain could see Lórcan was trying hard to find his way clear to a victory. He had only two more moves before he'd be forced to concede the game to Tnúthgal's challenge. He wiped at his face with a hand.

Lórcan reached out and moved another white pawn, then cursed once more.

Tnúthgal grinned and swept in, moving a black piece and removing another of Lórcan's.

The mood in the hall had grown grim. Eowain wanted to curse. He could see the move himself. There, a white stone could be moved to the fourth ring. One of Tnúthgal's pieces would be captured and the challenge defeated. But Lórcan needed time to see it.

The Lady Fidelm, who'd kept silent through the long game, suddenly spoke up. "If I recall, Bres imposed a great tribute on the people, to pay off monsters he hadn't the courage to fight himself. He became known for his oppressive rule and lack of hospitality."

Tnúthgal gave her an angry glance, then glared at Eowain. "Even when Nudd was restored with his silver arm as if he were a whole new man, war and oppression continued. He eventually stepped down to the more vigorous Trógain." Tnúthgal shrugged. "But my point is simply that sometimes in fickle, one must recognize defeat. Nudd knew when he was beaten."

"The game's not finished yet." Eowain felt frustrated and helpless. He could see the move, but it wasn't up to him to make it.

Lórcan stared at the board a long time. His eyes had become rheumy, and he rubbed at them. *Surely, the pain must be fierce,* Eowain thought.

The whole of the court was leaning forward, studying the board. Coins were changing hands as bets were laid. Eowain wanted to shout at those betting against his brother. Once more, he felt the restraining hand of Medyr on his arm.

"Enough of this." Eowain stood. "Clearly, the king is unwell. It's unfair to continue the match."

Tnúthgal leaned back with a satisfied air. "Then let him concede. I have him beat, we can all see that."

"Hardly. He has merely to—."

Lórcan reached out a hand to Eowain, grabbing his forearm. "It's alright, Eowain. Tnúthgal is right. Unwell or not, I chose to play. I must finish the game."

The king grimaced at Tnúthgal. "I concede, cousin. Well-played." Lórcan reached out a hand in friendship.

Tnúthgal took the hand with ill-grace. "It's about time. We could all see you were struggling. I'm surprised you didn't give up an hour ago."

Eowain helped his brother to his feet. "It's not in our nature to give up without a fight, cousin. You would do well to remember that."

•　•　•

There was a half-moon, hazed over and waning, but giving a little light on the village of Dúnsciath. They went carefully, four figures shrouded in black and cloaked against the winter chill. They kept on the track away from the river as fast as they dared over the rough ground. At last the track turned steeply uphill toward the crest of a hill where the old High King's Road crossed their path. But they took not the well-worn road, continuing instead on the track. The going became easier and ran straight northeast, and though broken here and there and weedy, it was in reasonable repair. After a while, the sky cleared, and a few stars showed.

Medyr knew the track and they made fair speed. Soon, they reached the western edge of an oval-shaped hill. Atop this plateau sat a circular mound, surrounded by a ditch wider and deeper than a tall man. The mound itself was steep and unnaturally regular, taller than Medyr and his companions. Brittle winter grass covered the mound, the ditch, and all the hill. It whispered in the night's gentle breeze, and Medyr shivered. In the moonlight, he could see the five hillocks that dotted the plateau just to the east of the mound. Beyond, a field of stones tilted more or less upright at odd angles, like three rows of broken teeth. To Medyr's eyes, wisps of fog and moonlight seemed to move among those stones like stalking cats.

He and his three companions, acolytes under his tutelage, moved withershins, leftwise, around the mound. It was forbidden to go the other way, though that was the shorter way from the trail. When they had come near three-quarters around the circle, Medyr gestured with a hand. The acolytes made themselves busy in the space between the large mound and the scattering of hillocks, unpacking gear from sacks they'd brought for the purpose.

While they worked, Medyr turned to face the mound. There was an opening there in the turf. A lintel of rough stones unbound by mortar surrounded a dark passage into the depths of the hill. No one knew how long ago it had been built, that mound and its passage. It was said it had stood there when Men first came to the land more than a thousand years ago. It was said to be haunted. It was said a tribe of Shynn still dwelt within, biding 'til the worlds should end.

Medyr knew something of the truth of it. Something, but hardly all. There was something to the tales. And yet more truth that he dared not imagine. Though it seemed nothing more than a grass-grown solitude, neither sheep nor kine nor beast nor fowl of the field was ever seen upon its height.

The acolytes kindled incense. The wormwood smoke, with a scent like leaves burnt in autumn, wafted through the winter night. Medyr breathed deeply of it, then joined them in preparing the ground. A wide circle of flour was poured upon the ground, and another of powdered silver was circumscribed within. A copper bowl, new-made that day with three carven *coelbreni* runes upon it, was laid within those concentric rings by the smoking incense. He filled it with lustral water from the sacred spring at Avainnglyn.

Medyr was careful with the preparations, recalling them from years of study. Into the bowl of water he dropped a bit of smoky quartz. It glittered in the waning moonlight as it plunked against the bottom of the bowl. He muttered a soft prayer, intoning the syllables with exactitude.

The lustral water burst abruptly into unnatural flame.

Medyr gestured for the acolytes to remain within the circle of flour, but beyond the circle of silver. Then he lifted the bowl with care. It was not hot, nor even warm. The flames flickered teal and jade within. *And the bowl must be lain between the Circles, facing the Northeast. And thy vestments should be black, and thy cap black. And the Sword must be at hand, but not yet in the ground. And it must be the Darkest Hour of the Night. And there must be no light, save for the bowl of lustral Fire. And the Conjuration of the Three must be made . . .*

It was known that spirits mingled invisibly with Men. This was taken for granted, no fool would contest it, Medyr knew. Good spirits and holy men like himself were responsible for divine inspiration. Inexplicable good fortune was often the work of benign mysteries. But just as the agents of the Gods moved freely in the world, so too did destructive forces of evil, bringing ill-fortune, disease, and madness. It was against these that the preparations had to be made with the utmost care.

He returned to the inner circle of powdered silver and began to chant.

•   •   •

IT WAS MORNING in the king's office of the tower. Medyr was there, his face blackened with soot and lined with weariness. "I have it on good authority, Lord Eowain."

"But you don't have proof."

"I have it from a Watcher tasked with looking after your cousin."

Eowain shook his head. The king was resting in the next room, and he didn't want to raise his voice, but his frustration with the Lord-Drymyn had grown dangerous. "We need more than the word of what very well may be nothing more than a figment of your imagination."

Medyr looked somewhat hurt by his accusation. But he shrugged and nodded. "Good. Good for you, lad. Skepticism is good. Quite right, yes, quite right you are. We can't arrest him. Not on the evidence of a specter. But mind me well, young lord. Your cousin Tnúthgal is plotting against you. He knows your brother's a cripple. He intends to start a smear campaign to woo your clients away from you."

"My clients? I'm not the king."

"No, but you're a candidate." *Medyr* tone was slow and deliberate. "If Tnúthgal can woo clients from you and from Lórcan, all he needs do is expose Lórcan's disability and call for a vote. But he daren't try while both the King's Company and your own clients are all loyal to you."

Eowain resented the tone of his voice, as though he were a still a small boy at his lessons. "A loyalty we will not lose."

"Won't you? Have you heard the reports from last night?"

Eowain nodded. "I have."

"A crew of bandits committed a rape—."

"—Our patrol chased them off."

Medyr cocked an eyebrow at him. "Oh, did they? When they chased them off, the people of the poor girl's thorp attacked your patrol."

The crook of Eowain's jaw clenched. "They—."

Medyr didn't let it go. "Attacked by their own people, Eowain. The King's Company attacked by their own people in their own land. People who should be loyal to their king. The chief-holder of Careganath has always been a friend to your father and your brother."

"Medyr—."

"As the people lose their faith in the king and his officers, the king's officers will lose faith in their king."

"That's enough!" He couldn't help it, he raised his voice and shook his head. "I won't let that happen."

Medyr threw his hands in the air. "It's already happening, will ye or nill ye, lad. When Lórcan's condition is revealed and it becomes known how we've conspired with the Lady Rathtyen to conceal it? That will play straight into Tnúthgal's plot. Eowain, you must stand now for the kingship and address yourself to Tnúthgal's inevitable challenge head on."

"There is no reason my brother can't be king."

"The law won't allow it." He slapped his forehead with the palm of his hand. "The people won't allow it. I won't be able to allow it. I have clear instructions in this matter from my own superiors in the Order. I'm not to allow Lórcan to hold the throne as a cripple, and I'm to encourage you to take the throne. The *coelbreni* and the portents of the birds and the clouds favor you."

Eowain frowned at Medyr. "How can you be so sure? Why is this knowledge of yours not witchcraft and superstition, like the reformationists say? How can it be trusted? We don't know what these spirits you converse with are."

Medyr scowled at the mention of reformation, but Eowain didn't care. For a generation already, there'd been calls from monks and nobles throughout the Five Kingdoms for the local Circle of the Drymyn Order to be reformed. The current superior was a proponent for the traditional ways, but the last head of Medyr's brotherhood had been a force for such reformation.

The Lord-Drymyn mastered himself. "My lord, your lack of faith disturbs me. Tnúthgal is sharking together lawless resolutes from the borderlands with the promise of food and plunder. We're going to see more of these bandit attacks, and soon."

PART SIX

THE NEXT DAY, Eowain rode with the Lady Fidelm's company back to the border-fort at Trígrianna. Eowain led a strength of some fifty-odd men from the King's Company, along with the Lady Fidelm's own entourage of cavalry and foot-soldiers. The noblewoman had eschewed the slow-moving wagon in which she'd arrived, opting instead to ride a-horse as the men did. She wore a studded-leather breastplate as if accustomed to it. When Eowain showed his concern, her reply was curt. "I grew up in Dolgallu, a remote village. Women there learn to fight as well as any man. A fact to which you should become accustomed if you look forward to my niece for a bride." He had to admit, she seemed well at ease with the broad sword at her hip.

By day's end, they were at Trígrianna. It was little more than a cattle-enclosure on a hill staring out into the rising forested hills of the savage Cailech tribe that stood beyond Droma's border to the northeast.

There'd been no reports of banditry since the defilement. Eowain had since learned the name of the girl: Eneuawg. A common girl, but illegitimate. As the truth of it turned out, her fellow villagers had offered her to the bandits. They'd bought the safety of their farm and their livestock with her virtue.

That was why they'd turned on the King's Company. They were afraid the bandits wouldn't honor their agreement once their sport was interrupted.

Eowain shook his head at the thought. That common people should have more faith in paying ransom to bandits than in the king's own men. *What is the world coming to?* He was more afraid than he'd been in a long time.

From Trígrianna, the Lady Fidelm insisted on continuing through Cailech territory, despite the late hour. "These bandits that have accosted your land." She gestured away toward the shadowed winter hills. "They are not Cailech men. Not yet. We put a particular scare into them before I agreed to come here, and obtained sureties that they would grant me safe passage. But these bandits? They are of your people's own making." She put a hand on Eowain's shoulder. "It's been good to see you, Eowain. You are missed at the court of Ardgar in Ivearda." She leaned close to him. "Do what must be done. Take the kingship of your people and set your kingdom back to rights. I'll take the details of our discussions back with me to Ardgar. I know time is important, I'll do what I can to return an answer quickly."

Eowain shook his head. "I don't like you or your men riding into Cailech territory after dark. If you're going to insist on this, we'll accompany you somewhat, until the light fades." Eowain made good on that promise.

Thus the Lord Eowain found himself with his drymyn and fifty-odd men of Droma returning through the wild borderlands as the gloaming spread across the face of the world. They had escorted the Lady Fidelm somewhat through Cailech territory, turning back only when they risked being caught in those lands after dark. Lady Fidelm and her men had taken their leave at the trot after wishing them a speedy return.

It was rough terrain, twisted with hills short but steep. He watched the winter forest as he rode. The dwindling sun in the west gave no warmth. His breath misted white in front of his face, frosting his moustache and the black fox fur lining his hood. He was glad that his helmet hung at his pommel. His shirt of steel-ringed mail and leather held the cold and it radiated through his coat and all the layers of wool, silk, and linen beneath. Even the saddle felt cold, as though his pale dapple gelding was made of frozen cream. The helmet would have mazed his mind.

Winter had come late that year, and with a vengeance. From the heat of summer to the heart of winter in less than a month. The leaves that had lingered through the autumn had frozen before they could change color. They glistened in the fading sun like strange shards of ice-coated malachite.

The horses of the ten arms-men around him occasionally stamped a hoof in the knee-deep snow. It had been a long ride that far, and they had yet farther to go. Dark clouds rolled through the sky to the northward. He didn't need his weather-wise drymyn to tell him the temperature would plummet before nightfall. They had to be under the shelter of Trígrianna before then.

Beside the ten a-horse, he had forty-four of foot, including twenty men of the king's own guard. They had returned nigh on three miles through the gloom and the cold when he saw the unexpected red-golden blaze of a fire through the trees. A large fire, where a large fire ought not to be.

Apprehension clutched at Eowain's throat. He spurred his horse and the mounted lancers with a cry. The drymyn Medyr whipped his pony to keep up, but the elite bodyguard and archers on foot soon fell behind despite their triple-time pace.

Eowain shouted clarion-clear over the pounding hooves of the mad chase. "Medyr, stay close!" He might have need of the damned drymyn's sorcery before much longer. As he raced ahead of his men, Eowain clung to the back of his gelding. The forest was grown dark now, and the trail was not well-kept in Cailech lands. Branches lashed him across the face. Roots, stones, and holes were hazards better taken slowly and by daylight, but he had no time for such concerns. He gave the gelding its head and hugged its neck, trusting it not to turn a fetlock.

Then he broke out from the dark forest into the cleared farmland. As he feared, the huts of Trígrianna burned on the hill ahead.

To his left and down a steep hill was the lake of Lyntrigrian, opaque in the hill's shadow. Peasants had already formed a bucket brigade from the lake to the village but he could see the effort was in vain. Their homes were all but lost.

He galloped around a wild curve of the trail and on through the village. He saw a child's burnt stocking lying in the mud. A hoarse prayer to Trógain escaped his lips.

Then ahead was the cattle enclosure, atop the highest point of the hill and defended by a stout log palisade. From within could be heard the frantic lowing of the cattle. From over the walls rose flights of spears and rocks, lobbed west into the darkness. There was a great shouting of men.

PART SEVEN

EOWAIN'S CAVALRYMEN STALLED before the small fort. Down the hillside, a large gang of bandits was fleeing away to the northwest. He let them go. Darkness would catch them before he ever did.

More of their kind were trapped, dead or dying, on the slopes of Trígrian hill. As Medyr caught up with him, Lord Eowain pointed to that field of agony. "I ordered some work done at Trígrian this past week." He looked at Medyr. "Will the Gods forgive me?"

Medyr looked over the screaming men. Man-traps had been concealed, just large and deep enough to trap a man's leg at the knee.

Medyr's voice was quiet. "Barbed?"

Lord Eowain nodded.

Medyr's face was grim. "They're smeared with shit?"

Lord Eowain nodded. "As you said."

"Their wounds will fester." He rubbed at this face with a hand.

From within the palisade came a ragged cheer. The danger had been driven off by Lord Eowain and his cavalry, and Eowain's own men responded with a volleying cheer of their own.

Medyr shook his head. "No. The Gods will never forgive either of us. But the Gods, they are forgetful."

• • •

MEDYR WORKED THROUGH all the rest of the night. He tended the wounds of farmers, herders, craftsmen, soldiers, and bandits all alike, and the bandits with shit in their wounds were tended first.

A lot of men lost limbs that day. Medyr mixed and administered many sleeping draughts and infusions for the alleviation of pain or senses. He sawed off many legs broken by Eowain's man-traps. And he prayed all throughout to the Gods of his people. He prayed for the alleviation of men's suffering, and to calm men's fears, and to heal their wounds.

But the Gods, they are forgetful. "Sometimes mercy and a quick end are the best we can offer." He administered the poisons himself to those beyond saving. He closed the staring, fear-stricken eyes of a boy barely old enough to carry wood.

• • •

WHEN EOWAIN ACCOMPANIED the Lady Fidelm into the Cailech hills, he'd left a strong force of seventeen men behind in the village. He'd suspected that either Trigrianna or another settlement near it might be the victim of the next attack, if not the Lady Fidelm's progress itself. If these bandits were motivated by his cousin, it made sense that they would strike at Fidelm's progress or at clients who supported Lórcan.

The bandits had had maybe twenty men. They'd left with no more than twelve. They'd also had some captives and camp-followers with them during their attack on the fort. These had been abandoned when they fled, and Eowain's men had taken them for captives. Eowain summoned Medyr once the wounded and the village fires were handled and together they questioned these prisoners.

"Peddlers, is it?" Eowain felt taciturn in the light of the burning brazier. The self-proclaimed peddler and his son and cousins were sitting on their knees in the mud, cowering. They seemed ill-used, whether by the bandits or Eowain's own men. They had nothing more for clothing than what Eowain's men had just provided to them, and that little more than rags and scraps for decency's sake. They'd all been burly men once, Eowain could see that, but now they were filthy and wretched.

"I swear 'tis jus' so, m'lord. Just 'onest peddlers. Friends of yer aunt, we is, my lord. 'Ad 'er sign onner wagon afore these fieves made off wif it." He spoke through missing front teeth and gestured indignantly in random directions. "I'm telling ye, me name is Kerron. Dis is me son Bithek and me cousins. We was workin' da King's High-Road not two weeks past. Sout' toward Dúnsciaf from Midachaf, we was peddlin'. Just shy of Monóc 'ill, we was, when dey come'd outta da trees an' took us, see?"

The other five were young men, not much older than fourteen summers. They were quiet, half-starved, terrified.

The speaker, Kerron, was two or more decades older and grizzle-haired. He groveled for mercy and freedom.

Eowain rolled his eyes. Judging by the accent, they weren't only peddlers, but Travelers, nomadic horse-traders, thieves, and pickpockets. "Let's say I believe you. Where'd they take you, these bandits? Where were they before they came here?"

"Kenna say if I knows fer sure, my lord. But fey dinna take us far from Monóc 'ill afore we was in a camp of 'em..." He warmed to his story-telling. Eowain shook his head. It would be days before he'd be able to get anything useful out of them.

• • •

EOWAIN LED MEDYR and his company of warriors back to Dúnsciath the next morning. The peddler Kerron and his son Bithek and their assorted relations traveled in the baggage train under guard, and one of Eowain's men continued to work with them to get their story. Among there many vices, Travelers were notorious for the ceaselessness of their storytelling, which involved wild flights of fancy, bold embellishments, and detailed family histories of any other tinkers involved. Rumor had it a Traveler had once spoken for an entire year without taking nary a breath.

When they at last arrived at Dúnsciath, a strange delegation had arrived ahead of him. There must have been nigh on a hundred men preparing camp on Dúnsciath's winter pastures when Eowain came in sight of them.

He rode ahead with his cavalrymen to meet these visitors, with Medyr to accompany him.

The drymyn whispered with Eowain as they approached. "That's the livery of Mórcant, king of the Hanlainn tribe."

Eowain's reply was terse, nodding to another banner. "And of his chief marshall."

"You sent word to King Mórcant?" Medyr seemed surprised.

"I did. He's king of the Airthir Federation. Last I checked, we were still of the Airthir Federation." No tribe existed as an island. Each was intimately involved in alliances and feuds with the others. Tribes like Droma gathered together with their allies into greater kingdoms, like the Kingdom of Airthir of which Mórcant of Hanlainn was chief. "We can avoid all of this unpleasantness about abdication with a strong show of force from Mórcant in support of Lórcan," continued Eowain. "Tnúthgal would never be able to raise a force of bandits so large or commit it to wait so long against a superior force with strong supplies in winter." He looked at the drymyn riding beside him. "Lórcan isn't a bad king, Medyr. Droma is reasonably well-stocked for the winter. We can wait them out a week or two, and the bandits will melt away in search of easier pickings, no matter what Tnúthgal might have promised them." Eowain gestured to the leaden grey skies, full of snow waiting to fall. "With a few hard days weather, they'll break, while we sit under canvas and timber."

Medyr shook his head. "You're putting much faith in Mórcant's support of your father's house. Your father caused a lot of difficulty for him in defying the king at Aileach, and died rather too conveniently soon. Mórcant never did have his revenge." Medyr puffed thoughtfully on his clay pipe, and the smell of linden leaf rose about him in a cloud. "I would beware of Mórcant's marshall." He pointed with the stem of the pipe. "He has a strong force here, and I fear they're not altogether friendly."

Eowain saw then what the drymyn meant. Though their master's emblem proclaimed them to be men of the Lord-Marshall of King Mórcant, much of the livery among the soldiers identified them as men of the Khaibe tribe to Droma's south. The Khaibe were another of Droma's voracious neighbors, a rival and unwilling ally in the Airthir Federation.

Eowain felt doubt gnaw at his gut. King Mórcant of Hanlainn to the southwest was the strongest of the four tribes of Airthir, and commanded military service from each of his three erstwhile allies. He'd chosen to send a force of their rivals into their kingdom to camp at the foot of Scíath hill, upon which stood the fort of their King. Eowain realized this might not be a delegation so much as the beginning of a siege.

Eowain ground his back teeth together. "Indeed," he said slowly. "They might have sent back a troop of those Droma men we pay up as tribute every month."

"Aye, might have. But didn't." Medyr lifted his chin up to the fort, puffing on his pipe.

Eowain understood the gesture and figured quickly. "We have about twenty men up there. Ten here with me. Twenty-seven of foot behind me, plus the rabble of our entourage." Eowain raised an eyebrow at the drymyn.

"Scoff-law." Medyr cuffed him on the knee with a smile. "So sixty-odd men against, how many would you say, my Lord-Captain?"

"Thirty mounted. About fifty of foot. And a baggage train."

"Call it a hundred then?"

"Aye." Eowain didn't like those odds at all. They could hold the fort, he didn't doubt, but a field battle would be a disaster.

An approaching delegation of ten men afoot came out from the camp, armed with spears and shields. Three more men stood together behind them.

"Good luck." Medyr whispered as they came within earshot.

Eowain smirked at the drymyn, then proclaimed himself. "I am Eowain son of Findtan—!"

•   •   •

THE LORD-MARSHALL of Hanlainn met peaceably with the Lord-Captain of Droma and was welcomed into the Tower of Donnghal. An immediate audience with King Lórcan was organized. Medyr and Eowain escorted the Lord-Marshall, as did the Lord-Marshall's lieutenant, an ugly and brutish Khaibe tribesman of some reputation by the name of Daimine.

At the center of the hall of Dúnsciath between the two great fireplaces, the Lord-Marshall stood and shook his head. At the king's table Lórcan, Eowain, and the Lady Rathtyen sat. Standing against the far wall were the officers of the king: the king's chamberlain, his master-of-field, his master-of-the-hunt, the constable of Dúnsciath, and the Lord-Drymyn.

The Lord-Marshall shook his head again. "Great-King Mórcant cannot support a crippled man upon the throne of Droma. Nor can he favor one candidate for your kingdom over another." He looked over the assembled court of Lórcan, then paced about the hall in the firelight. "By law, the choice must be made by the people of Droma. If you fear you don't command the votes of enough of your clients, then perhaps you shouldn't command their lands?"

Lórcan stood and waved his bandaged, crippled hand in the direction of the village green, where the Lord-Marshall's men were making camp. "And all those men?"

The Lord-Marshall shrugged. "They are to leave with me in the morning to return to Hanlainn territory downriver."

Lady Rathtyen stood as well. "So Mórcant will leave us to swing, will he? After all the treasure my late husband, rest his soul, brought Mórcant's way up-river?"

Lórcan banged a fist on the table. "And announce not just to

Tnúthgal and Ninnid, but to the Khaibe as well that we can't depend on your support."

The Lord-Marshall shook his head. "It's not *me*, Lórcan, I'm only the messenger." He made mock of innocence. "These are King Mórcant's wishes. It's only through *my* support that I'm not come to dispossess you of your throne." He waved a negligent hand at black-clad Rathtyen. "Mórcant's had enough of your aunt's manipulations, with her treasure and her river trade. Too many weapons have been passing north, we've noticed. Smugglers, no doubt."

Aunt Rathtyen's eyes went suddenly wide, then she coughed demurely and sat once more. "Hmm. No doubt, I'm sure." It seemed to Eowain as if she wished to sink into the floor of a sudden.

Lórcan turned to look at her with thunder in his eyes. "What have you done?"

She shook her head. "It was nothing." She waved the matter away with a hand. "A small business transaction. A favor from an old friend." A trace of a smile crossed her lips for a moment, then she looked at Lórcan and grew serious. "He sent us a shipment of weapons, a few weeks ago."

Eowain turned to her now as well. "What shipment of weapons?" She shook her head.

Lórcan growled at her. "Tell me, old woman."

"Crossbows. From the sea-markets in Difelin. Foreigner-made."

"Where are they?"

"Lost. They were lost on the river." She pointed to the Lord-Marshall. "In Hanlainn territory. Four weeks ago."

Eowain remembered hearing something of it, news of a river barge from Rathtyen's little trade flotilla that had been lost. It had been passing between Gruiniath and Hanlainn territory when bandits from the haunted hills across the river in Gruiniath had seized it. But no one had mentioned it carried a shipment of arms.

Eowain groaned. Lórcan put his face in his good hand.

"What, what is it?" Rathtyen looked from Lórcan to Eowain and back.

Eowain knew what his brother must also have thought. If the shipment had been sold up the river to Tnúthgal or the Ivea tribe, and there were enough starving men in the hills willing to fight for food, then all that was needed was to give them those weapons and a cause in which to use them.

Medyr spoke up. "My lady, you have given your enemies the weapons with which to unseat you, and the will to do so. If Lórcan won't abdicate and allow an election, Tnúthgal and Ninnid will have the men and the weapons they need to challenge us." He paused and pointed his pipe stem at their visitor. "And Mórcant won't stop them from doing it."

The Lord-Marshall sneered. "It wouldn't be legal for anyone to support a cripple for the throne. Farewell, Lórcan Half-Hand."

PART EIGHT

LATER THAT SAME NIGHT, Eowain's men pieced together the peddler's story. Eowain consulted with Lórcan, Medyr, and Rathtyen over his tale and other reports. Everything pointed to a possible location for the bandit camp in which the peddler and his sundry relations had been held. Reports suggested there might be as many as forty men in that camp, so Eowain wanted sixty. The word went out quietly by messenger. Through the night, a strong force of the King's men were to gather from the countryside at the thorp of Gormlyn some two and a half miles east from Dúnsciath.

As the first glimmerings of dawn burned behind the head of distant Mount Ydrys like a halo, the frosty morning air sighed down from the mountains. Chill fog rolled through the hills of Droma toward the river and the lowlands and the distant sea far beyond.

The next morning, the Lord-Marshall and his gang of Khaibe soldiers prepared to return south. They took advantage of King Morcant's right to coyne-and-livery and provisioned themselves from Dúnsciath's larders before they left. Rather too well, in Eowain's opinion. Not only would Mórcant not support Lórcan, but it seemed his men had orders to strip him of as many supplies as they could carry.

Before the sun was quite up, the Lord-Marshall's men broke

camp and marched away south, a plain sign to any spies in the country that Mórcant would neither support nor oppose Lórcan. Droma
was on its own in this matter.

That suited Eowain just fine. Though he'd hoped for Mórcant's
support and a quick end to the question of his brother's abdication,
their new intelligence gave him hope that they could now finish this
on their own. No sooner had Mórcant's men marched away south
than Eowain arrayed his own small troop and rode out on the east
trail at a hurried pace. At the thorp of Gormlyn, he met the men
he'd summoned, assembled as ordered. From there, he rode his
chariot at the head of a column of nigh on seventy men, and the
Lord-Drymyn Medyr accompanied them on a stout pony.

By a circuitous route through the hills north of the Drægan
ridge, Eowain made his way past the village of Dúngráig, then north
through Echraivaile and Heddooch before circling west toward
Careganath. But then he turned his men off the trail not a mile
distant from that settlement.

Instead Eowain ordered his troops into the woods, with cavalry
to the rear as a reserve. He dismounted the chariot, and with two
score infantry bearing spears, swords, and bows, he advanced with
them on a line to the north through the forest.

The rolling hills there were already chaotic enough, studded
with ash and silver birch as they were. But thorn and bracken conspired to choke the narrow ways between hills and under trees, and
their footing was cloaked with treacherous snow. Eowain's breath
frosted on the morning air. He rubbed the icy rime from the
tips of his moustaches with the back of his gloved hand. His toes
ached with cold in his boots, despite woolens and good leather.
He griped and grumbled to himself like any soldier as he scanned
the trees ahead.

They'd gone not more than a mile when the land began rising
abruptly toward the oak-crowned summit of Maladarach hill. The
morning light crowned over the head of distant Ydrys at last, casting
bolts of misty light and long shadows through the trees.

Eowain cocked his head. Had that been the creaking of a branch he'd heard?

There was a strong, ringing sound as if a harp string had been plucked. A thud echoed through the trees as one of his men jerked backward and fell to the ground with an arrow protruding from his skull.

Shouts went up all along the line as men brought shields to bear against the sudden onslaught.

A dozen or more bandits sniped at them from the trees. Eowain and his men spread out and advanced on the line, tree to tree, but the bandits scampered away, falling back, refusing to be engaged.

The man next to Eowain screamed and went down as his leg disappeared under him into the snow. Down the line to his right, another man was jerked up by a rope into the trees.

Eowain's jaw clenched with fury. The bastards had set traps and deadfalls to cover their retreat. Helpless, he heard and saw more of his men falling victims to leg-holds, snares, and pit-traps. It was a grisly advance up the hill of Maladarach, and Eowain cursed when he heard the hurried flight of horses' hooves before ever they reached the little farm atop the hill.

Later, Eowain watched helplessly, shaking his head while Medyr and his acolyte treated the wounded. "They used crossbows and had light steeds waiting. There were traps set."

Medyr considered this as he tightened a splint around the leg of a man who'd been rendered senseless with herb-magick. "It seems to me like they retreated down a well-executed escape route?"

Eowain grimaced and nodded. "They knew we were coming."

By midday, Eowain and Medyr stood together outside an old, ruined barn. There had proven to be a hidden cellar beneath the basement. It was a sordid-smelling place where the bandits had camped.

Bran the Handsome, chief-holder of the thorp at Maladarach, seemed not at all surprised to learn that an abandoned barn on his property had been hosting a conclave of villains for weeks.

Bran was on his knees, held by two of Eowain's men. "You knew about this."

"They threatened my family." Bran seemed calm. "Who'm I supposed to trust, after the rape over in Careganath? You and your men?" He didn't seem convinced.

"How many?"

"I'm not sure. Maybe forty or fifty. They moved around a lot. A dozen here, two dozen there, coming and going."

"Mounts?"

"About two dozen, well-kept."

"Yours."

Bran sneered. "They're thieves, ain't they? Hells yes, they're mine."

"Held you to ransom for your own good behavior, did they?" Eowain didn't feel convinced. The hidden cellar certainly wasn't new. Eowain didn't believe the bandits had stolen horses or anything else from Bran.

"What was I supposed to do, Eowain? You ain't king yet, and we ain't seen hide nor hair from Lórcan in nigh on a month. Just you, parading that foreigner woman to and from Cailech. Is that the idea now, we'll start crowing in the wilderness with those savages?"

Eowain knelt down to look him in the eye. "Where'd they get the crossbows, Bran?"

"Couldn't tell you if I knew."

Eowain didn't believe him. Bran knew, he was certain, but was more afraid of the bandits than of his own king. "You're too good-looking for me to ask again, Bran." Eowain gestured to the two soldiers holding him. "Tell me. Before the lads have to hurt you."

He shook his head.

"Bran?" Eowain was losing his patience. Maybe his men could tell, or maybe they were angry about the ambush. One of his soldiers wrenched at Bran's arm.

The chief-holder relented with a squawk. "Alright! Aiii, alright, I said! Stranger come round here a few weeks ago with a wagon. Come down the road from Monóc hill, looking for someone, I don't know who." Bran waved to the eastern trail. "He wandered off again with his wagon toward Ruakhavsa and Bankern. I never did know what he was hauling in that wagon, but he had five surly-lookin' lads with him what had them cross-bow things."

Eowain rose and stepped away from Bran. He crooked a finger for Medyr to join him, then turned away from Bran to whisper. "What do you think? That peddler Kerron and his cousins, work-ing the High-King's Road two weeks' past?"

Medyr shrugged. "The timing makes sense. The shipment that your aunt was bringing up river, hijacked from Hanlainn territory on its way north? The sudden appearance of crossbows in the hands of bandits? So much for the innocent peddler and his distant relations."

Eowain turned back to look at the chief-holder. The thorp of Bran the Handsome wasn't one of the larger hold-fasts. Fifty-odd souls on forty-odd acres. With good seed and no troubles, they could turn a decent profit come harvest time. They had a small grain mill that served the settlements nearby, and a modest tailor who did good work with woolen kersey and serge. Bran's wife had brought a handful of horses to the hold as part of her dowry, and he'd made good custom from breeding and foaling since she'd passed on. Bran's son was serving honorably in the King's Com-pany, as his father had before him. Altogether, it was a respectable place, and Eowain would have been glad to count its people among his clients.

But Bran had been a gadfly for years, first under Findtan's reign, and then under Lorcán's. Maladarach was a border hold-ing, and after the wars with Ivea a generation earlier, that border had crept ever closer. Bran agitated for a campaign to retake the hill three miles to the north that his grandfather had once held.

Bran complained that not enough trade from the High-King's Road came to his little thorp. Bran caviled that there was never enough relief for farmers when the harvests were bad, nor enough subsidy when the harvests were good.

Frankly, Eowain despised Bran. And now, he also knew him as his cousin's not-so-secret partisan. But he still had an obligation to the people who lived there, to keep them safe. As much as he might want to carve the pretty off Bran's famously handsome face, the people of Maladarach wouldn't be any safer, and their opinion of Eowain and his brother might turn yet further away. Was it better in this case to show mercy or strength?

There was a sound like the sizzle of water on a hot oven. *What's that?* Eowain looked to the two men holding Bran, then to left and right, and even behind. One of the men seemed to hear it too and shrugged at him. It sounded as if it were nearby, yet also as if it were moving, but he couldn't see anything to account for it.

Then, quite suddenly, a flame appeared with a pop between Eowain and Bran. There was no firebrand, no live coal, not even a cinder. Simply a disembodied flame, hovering alone in that morning of the winter, as far from the ground as the head of a young boy at play.

Eowain gawked, he couldn't help himself. It danced random and erratic through the air. He knew he should do something, but didn't know what. First it was here, then it was yon, then thither and there. It flickered as it went, like a candle in the wind.

The men holding Bran went pale with fright. Bran himself went grey.

Then the dancing flame collided with one of Eowain's men and kindled the tartan of his livery. All of them stared at the coruscating flickers as the flame bobbed away. The man slapped once, twice, and again at the tongues of fire licking along the warp and weft of his woolen tartans. He released his hold on Bran the Handsome, swatting with both hands at the spreading conflagration. He began to scream like a pig at slaughter, flailing like a fool as he fled from the very thing he was wearing.

The dancing flame weaved again and again through the air, a-lighting on clumps of dead winter grass, fallen twigs, and broken branches, spreading its flames out in a semi-circle between Eowain and Bran the Handsome.

The other soldier released Bran, removed his cloak, and beat at the burgeoning flames. Bran the Handsome shrieked and ran off into the forest.

Medyr stepped forward to face the flame, a far-away look in his eyes. Eowain dared not imagine what his drymyn saw beyond the pale of the world. Medyr raised his hands, gesturing with inscrutable purpose, then barked a single word: *"Forsendath!"*

The flame flared, wavered, then burst into sparks and vanished.

Medyr stumbled on his two legs, then fell to his knees in the snow.

The man on fire screamed as he ran. One of Eowain's men had the mercy to put a bolt through him before he reached the forest's edge and set the whole kingdom aflame.

PART NINE

THE NEXT DAY, the bonfire at Lord's Point Hill to the southeast was set a-light. According to the reports that came back, the settlement at Easavain Mills had been attacked. The locals had fought against bandits and driven them off with minor casualties and some damage to the mill. Some grain and flour had been stolen.

The day after that, a patrol from Dúnsciath to Scíthin was attacked by peasants in Cruinnmynn. The report claimed that the peasants' attack was incited by a gang of bandits leading them. Once again, Lórcan's own people had turned against the King's Company.

Over the next three days, reports continued to filter in. Heddooch was attacked, but the peasants fought with courage. An archer patrol in the southeastern forests led a surprise attack against a small hive of villains they discovered. One patrol observed a large force of bandits moving along the northeastern border, while another patrol was lured by a different band of brigands into a forest trapped with deadfalls.

Then out of the southeastern forests of the Hagan tribe came a nobleman traveling in disguise with two guards. The noble revealed himself to a patrol and commanded them to escort him to Dúnsciath.

When the notable arrived, he demanded an immediate audience with Medyr. Revealing himself to the Lord-Drymyn in his humble round-house in the village, the nobleman proved to be Dirmyg, a high-ranking member of Medyr's Order.

Medyr was surprised and gladdened by the unexpected visit. He greeted Dirmyg with a strong embrace and good beer while an acolyte prepared an evening meal for them.

"What brings you to Dúnsciath, my friend?"

Dirmyg had been the scion of a noble family in Larriocht before he'd joined the Order, and he sniffed at Medyr's humble accommodations. "This is how they keep you out here in the sticks, is it?"

"I like it well enough. It's quiet."

"Not as I hear it."

"I'm sure it's no surprise."

Dirmyg shrugged. "Tnúthgal's been chomping at the bit ever since Lórcan succeeded Findtan with the help of his aunt's money and connections. And Mórcant swore a blood oath against Findtan and all his sons when Findtan turned against the king at Aileach. You won't get aid from that quarter."

The acolyte served bowls of stew prepared according to the strict code of the drymyn's diet. Medyr stirred at the shallots, carrots, potatoes and rutabagas, mixing the garlic, thyme, and sage into the vegetable broth. "We know as much already." He took a bite of the stew and waved his spoon in a southwesterly direction. "You missed the Lord-Marshall by five days."

"My master Garanhon recommends you remove Lórcan as king and install his brother Eowain."

"I'm trying. Eowain is stubborn and loyal to his brother. He won't take the throne."

"Perhaps there are more... *decisive* measures you could take?"

"I've been tutor to these boys since they were old enough to walk."

"Nevertheless."

"I won't do it. The brothers or the people have to decide. I support the brothers in so far as I can, but I won't have the Order making kings in Droma. It's not our place."

"Then install Tnúthgal." Dirmyg seemed unflappable as he spooned the vegetable stew to his mouth.

"The *coelbreni* don't favor Tnúthgal. I have to think about the people here, not just the needs of kings and Gods." Medyr raised an eyebrow at his old friend. He'd changed much since they'd been acolytes together.

"Kings and Gods don't favor men. Tnúthgal is older, wiser. And he has powerful friends in Larriocht right now."

"Foreigners, you mean." Medyr sniffed at the suggestion.

"Not like you think. Not those sea-bitten barbarians from the north-countries. Sophisticated men of the Spirit, coming out of Aukriath."

"The Narician drymyn? With their minds full of wheels and cogs? No, thank you." Medyr squinted at his old friend. "I'm surprised you'd suggest as much. I didn't think your master supported the Narician reforms?"

Dirmyg shrugged over his soup. "My master's mind is not known to me on the matter, and I don't expect Tnúthgal would be a friend of reform. Not with so wise a mind as yours to guide him, Lord-Drymyn." He broke off a chunk of bread and dipped it in the soup. "But he has friends in Larriocht that would like to see him succeed. Friends with interests of their own in your little kingdom."

Medyr didn't like the turn of this conversation. He stiffened and scowled at his guest. "How long will you be staying?"

Dirmyg considered Medyr through narrowed eyes, then shrugged. "We'll leave in the morning, if that would please you."

• • •

OVER THE NEXT SEVERAL DAYS, encounters with the bandits increased. Eowain's patrols would ambush a raiding party of bandits, and bandits would ambush one of his own patrols in turn.

One troop would be peppered with bolts and arrows and spears from the grass or the trees, and forced to flee from bandits lest they be overwhelmed. Others would skirmish on the high-road or chase villains along the interior trails of the kingdom.

Then bandits mounted an assault against the ring-fort at Darachtír along the southwestern border of the kingdom. When the arrival of the King's men failed to frighten them off, a skirmish ensued. The warriors of the king were cut off and cut down. The bandits left one man alive to tell the tale.

Tensions were alive amongst the people as well. In the village of Dúnsciath, a duel between two freeholders ended in death. The man loyal to Lórcan did not survive, while the man loyal to Tnúthgal fled north to Greanvaile, one of Tnúthgal's clients. The chief-holder, Crimthann, refused to return the man to face the king's justice.

While these skirmishes punctuated Eowain's daily life and drew his attentions first one way then another, an invitation arrived at Dúnsciath. It was from Hanlainn, where Mórcant was king. Lórcan was expected to present himself to the king of the Airthir Federation.

"You have to go. It's not an invitation. It's an order." The king's chamberlain, a woman named Neued, read it aloud again to the council.

"If you leave, you'd have to take a strong force of our men with you." Eowain's patrols were already under constant pressure from the bandits. He couldn't seem to gain an advantage over them, and his men were stretched thin around the kingdom already.

Rathtyen shook her head. "If you leave with a force of men, Tnúthgal, Ninnid, and their 'bandits' will be at the gates of Dúnsciath before nightfall. Even if you leave a strong force here, Mórcant will hold you to ransom the kingship for Tnúthgal."

Medyr puffed on his pipe. "Indeed, you cannot answer your master's summons. You and your family will lose everything."

Eowain took his brother's arm. "They're right. You can't leave if the bandits are still a threat." He was already anxious. He'd come to the meeting with other news of his own. "And if you stay, you risk angering Mórcant and rousing the Hanlainn and the Khaibe against us. We need to eliminate the bandits as a threat. And I've just had news today that might let us end this."

• • •

EOWAIN GATHERED A STRONG company of men that night and left from Bankern at dawn. By midday, he was assaulting a small, wooded hill amid a marshy heath in the northeast wilderness.

Once more, he was too late. A mere skeleton crew had remained on the hill to taunt Eowain's men into a network of traps that did nothing but slow them down and bleed their strength. Before Eowain knew it, they'd escaped once more into the forests.

Nor was that his last failure to end their depredations. Another mission the next day met with strong opposition. The skirmish lasted most of an afternoon before the bandit force broke out and escaped.

So Eowain was in no good humor when another invitation arrived at Dúnsciath, this time addressed to him. It was from the drymyn Calcas, another high-ranking official within the Order. The messenger informed him that Calcas would be entering Droma from the southeast, sent no doubt from Ard-Cátha, where the leader of the Drymyn Order of the Five Kingdoms dwelt. Eowain was invited to meet with him at Mynnynrainsh, a cattle-farm at the northeast end of the Drægan ridge.

• • •

EOWAIN RODE THE NEXT morning from Dúnsciath with Medyr and about thirty of his warriors. As he traveled, a rider came over Dúngráig hill from the north. He wore the green, gold, and white livery of the Donnghaile clan, a scout, reporting back from patrols sent out in advance of Eowain's progress.

"There's a large gang of bandits, perhaps as many as twenty, moving southeast from the wild lands north of Maladarach and Ruakhavsa."

Eowain turned to Medyr. "Well that you advised me to send our engineers to Mynnynrainsh last night." He ordered his footmen to make their best speed toward Echraivaile in the northeast, then ordered his cavalry to triple their pace and rode on toward Mynnynrainsh at a gallop.

PART TEN

MYNNYNRAINSH WAS A WEALTHY farmstead at the north-eastern terminus of the Drægan ridge, held by the House of Domnall. They had seven fine horses, and a herd of more than one-hundred head of cattle. Their thorp supported about forty souls, and their position on the trail between Trígrianna and Dúnsciath allowed the thorp to trade their goods to other thorps and villages. Domnall, the chief of Mynnynrainsh, had always been a staunch supporter of Lórcan.

Eowain came thundering down the trail with his troop of cavalry. A large party of travelers was camped at the pond north of Mynynnrainsh. He rode down to greet them.

After identifying himself to the camp guards, he and Medyr were admitted to the tent of Calcas, Drymyn of the Order.

He was reading from a scroll when they were admitted. Simple camp furniture and a small cot were all that adorned the pavilion.

Calcas rose from his seat, setting the scroll aside. "Brother Medyr, it is good to see you again." He embraced the Lord-Drymyn of Droma perfunctorily. "And Lord Eowain, thank you for coming."

"Your invitation didn't leave much room to refuse." Eowain looked over the drymyn. He was neither over-tall, nor under-short, and had a round, cheerful face. "What business brings you to Droma, Brother?"

"I'm told a coronation is to be performed?" He blinked at Eowain.

What nonsense is this? Eowain almost said as much, but bit his tongue. "Lórcan is still king in Droma."

Calcas looked puzzled. "Is he? I was told that you would be taking the throne?"

Eowain shook his head. "It seems everyone and their mother would like it thus, but so long as my brother draws breath, he is king in Droma."

Outside the tent, a hoarse shout went up among the men. Eowain had expected as much. He put a firm hand on Calcas's shoulder. "We had reports of a large bandit gang coming this way. How many men have you got here? I fear you may be in danger."

Calcas did not seem perturbed. "I have twenty mounted warriors and another fifty a-foot."

Eowain nodded. "If I might borrow your horsemen?"

Calcas nodded and waved him away as if his horsemen were of no consequence. "Of course, Lord Eowain."

"I hope to do more than chase them off, Brother." Eowain bowed and left. Through the tent flaps, Medyr watched as he swung up on to his horse. Eowain shouted for the cavalrymen to rally to him and they all charged away toward the north. Medyr and Calcas stepped out of the tent to watch.

Across an open field of hillocks and tall grass to the northwest, bandits charged at the camp. Four on light mounts had shields and spears, while another three on sturdier mounts behind them had shields and swords. On either flank rode two more riders on light horses. Behind the horsemen, a score of footmen were howling across the grassy hills with swords, spears, and bows.

Eowain and his thirty-odd men erupted from the camp, and the foremost bandits on their light horses panicked and swerved away. A few crossbow bolts shot across the grassy fields, but the rest swung around in a circle and fled back the way they'd come. The bandits on heavier mounts, however, couldn't hope to break off. Eowain and his troops outnumbered those ten-to-one and crashed upon them like a rock slide. Then he and his men rode on, trampling the score of rabble on foot into the ground as well.

It was over almost before it was begun. The survivors scattered, and Eowain and the Drymyn Calcas's men pursued them into the hills.

Medyr returned to the tent in conversation with Brother Calcas.

"—No one wants violence and bloodshed, Medyr. Least of all me."

"I'm well aware of your pacifism, but Lórcan and Eowain are under great pressure from their rivals." He gestured back toward the scene outside, exasperated. It vexed him that he'd not been informed that a superior of the Order was coming. "Crowning Eowain isn't enough anymore. His cousins will be howling for a fair election while their bandit gangs threaten his people. As much as I respect you, Brother, your peaceful ideals have no place here."

"Nevertheless, the King at Aileach cannot have Droma embroiled in a civil war over this election. There are rumors the King of Gruiniath might launch a spring campaign. The Gods want Eowain for the king of Droma, and the Gods don't lie."

Medyr shook his head. How could he make Calcas understand? "The Gods, they are forgetful, Brother." Vague oracular proclamations alone wouldn't make a king of Eowain without the support of the people.

But Calcas remained firm. "Eowain must take the kingship of Droma, and he must hold it."

Medyr tried again. "I don't disagree with you, Brother. Eowain is the fittest of the candidates, though he doesn't believe it himself. But to hold the throne is another matter. There will be those who disapprove of putting yet another unelected king on the throne, and a young and unmarried one at that. This bandit problem is going to get worse, even if Eowain becomes king. He needs a wife, and better yet a son, to quell any doubts."

"So get him married."

"We're trying, Brother. The Lady Fidelm of Dolgallu was here not a fortnight ago to discuss a marriage between her niece and Lord Eowain. But they insist that the girl must marry a king, and Eowain won't take the throne—."

There was a clatter outside the tent as Eowain and his riders returned from the skirmish. Eowain entered the tent with a jangle of armor. "Apologies for the interruption, Drymyn. I think we've scared them off. And I have two squads of infantry patrolling the hills between here and Echraivaile. If we're lucky, they'll run afoul of my men and we'll be done with them."

Calcas shook his head, reaching out to a brownish smear across the weft of Eowain's tartan. "So much bloodshed. It's shameful."

Eowain pulled the jerkin out to have a look at the stain and shrugged. "I regret that it's necessary, Drymyn. These bandits had intended to seize you for a ransom. And they've been a plague to our farms and cattle-herds for weeks already."

Calcas sniffed. "Kidnap and ransom a drymyn? Preposterous. Our very persons are sacrosanct. So it's always been."

Eowain removed his riding gloves and his helmet. "Kings may respect the sacred person of the drymyn, but bandits? I wouldn't wager on it. So come, Brother, tell me now. What is all this about, then?"

"As I said, I was sent to confirm you in the kingship of Droma."

"I've told you, I'm not the king of Droma. Lórcan is. And he'll remain king, so long as I have anything to say about it."

Calcas frowned at him. "This nonsense is going to continue, you do realize that? Lórcan can't be king, crippled as he is, and the Gods don't favor your cousins. That leaves just you. You must take the throne."

Eowain shook his head. "No. If that's all you came to say, Drymyn, then I'm afraid you've wasted your trip."

"Hrmph." Calcas snorted and crossed his arms. "I admire your loyalty to your brother. Go ahead, hasten back to Dúnsciath and defend him. It's futile though."

"It's only futile if I don't try. I've been saying as much to Medyr for days now." He shrugged. "As long as I've come all this way, I'll stop in and see the chief-holder here before we leave."

Medyr cleared his throat. "Drymyn Calcas and I have a bit more business to discuss. I'll join you again straightaway, Lord-Captain."

Eowain made his respect to Drymyn Calcas and departed.

"I told you," said Medyr. "He's as stubborn as his father and brother put together."

"So what of this wedding?"

Medyr shook his head. "We made a respectable offer of a bride-price, but they were adamant about the kingship. So far as any of them know, the whole point of the wedding is to settle an old feud and unite the Donnghaile and the Gwynn against the Cailech." He shrugged. "But without the authority of a king behind that alliance, it's worthless to the Gwynn. They need to know that Droma will send troops against the Cailech, and they can't trust that Tnúthgal or Ninnid will do so. They're both married already, and have no love for the Gywnn."

"And so?"

"Lady Fidelm took our proposals back to King Ardgar of Ivearda. We've heard nothing yet."

Brother Calcas stroked his chin for a moment. "Perhaps they could use some persuading? I think I can delay my business long enough for a detour to Ivearda, and an audience with King Ardgar."

Medyr bowed low. "You would have our gratitude, Brother."

"We shall see. Stay with Eowain. Keep him safe."

"Aye, Brother." With that, Medyr took his leave of Brother Calcas.

Medyr re-joined Lord Eowain as he concluded his own business with chief-holder Domnall of Mynnynrainsh. Eowain had struck a deal for fresh horses and a troop of men to bolster the King's Company, and the two were drinking a cup of ól to seal the agreement. Before long he ordered Medyr and the men of Droma to mount up for their return trip.

They weren't long on the trail before they met Eowain's foot-soldiers. Scattered packs of bandits had been encountered in the hills above Mynnynrainsh, fleeing back to their hidden camps in the north. "We showered 'em with arrows from a distance," reported the lieutenant of the troop, "and caught a handful what run afoul of some traps we laid for 'em. But the rest escaped, my Lord-Captain."

Disappointed and tired after another long day, Eowain and Medyr returned to Dúnsciath shortly after nightfall.

•   •   •

EOWAIN AND LÓRCAN, with their councilors about them, sat in the hall the next morning and heard still more reports from their patrols and debated what course of action to take next.

"Your Highness, we encountered a scouting party of bandits near Darachrith. They engaged our men with spears and arrows before melting away into the forest."

"Lord-Captain, our patrol in the southeast, we was attacked near Careganant. We rousted a small gang and chased them halfway to Cruinnmynn before the cowards disappeared into the woods."

"A large host was spotted on the march, heading north between Drúchtmil and Drochavaile. Our patrol was outnumbered and driven off by mounted archers with crossbows."

Lórcan put his face in his one good hand. "Will this never end?"

PART ELEVEN

EOWAIN SHOOK HIS HEAD. "How can it, brother? Our cousins know you're crippled, and they use the ancient laws to build resentment against you, pointing to the bandits as a sign of the evil your condition will bring down on the kingdom."

The king looked at his brother. "If I abdicate and there's an election, there's no guarantee you will be made king."

Eowain nodded. "Yes. I know."

"If you're not made king, chances are it will be Tnúthgal or Ninnid, neither of whom have much love for us. If they don't kill us outright, we could be banished."

Eowain shrugged. "Or they'll let us slink away to our own holding at Trígrianna to live out the rest of our days in peace?"

Lórcan snorted. "Not bloody likely. So long as they've got this gang of bandits on their payroll, no doubt they'll use them to turn us out of Trígrianna, first chance they get."

"They can try." Eowain grinned.

Lórcan shook his head again. "Whether I abdicate or not, we'll be fighting for our lives."

Medyr cleared his throat. "There is still the possibility of the marriage alliance with the Gwynn."

"What good would that do us? Near as I can tell from our scouts' reports, there are as many bandits roaming the kingdom as there are men in my own Company. Do you think they'll stop raiding at us just because Eowain's engaged to wed?"

"The people would see a married king as a good omen, a sign of stability in the king's house."

"I've been wed nigh on ten years, with three brats to show for it already. What stability has that brought?"

"It brought much stability while you were hale, Your Highness. Tnúthgal and Ninnnid dared not stir against you while you and your family enjoyed the love of the people." Medyr was seated at a corner of the hall, away from the table. "If we could show that Eowain was engaged to wed, and could give these bandits a solid trouncing, it would do much to reassure your supporters, and hearten the realm to resist these brigands."

Lórcan pushed away from the table and stood up. "Ardgal of the Gwynn isn't going to agree to any marriage that doesn't involve a king for a bridegroom." He paced away from the Lord-Drymyn. "And if Eowain claims the throne *de facto*, without the niceties of an election, Tnúthgal and Ninnid will hit us with everything they have. This is all still just the warning signs of trouble, I'll tell you."

Aed the Woodward nodded. "The king is right. Already, there are whispers in the King's Company. Desertion or mutiny cannot be far away."

Eowain stood up. "Lórcan, you know I will support you, whatever you decide. But our cousins can't be allowed to gain the throne. We'll lose everything. We have to hit them, now, with everything we have."

"We still have no solid proof that these bandits are their doing, brother."

"Yet we all know they are. Why should we wait any longer?" Eowain looked to the others for support. There were nods around the table. He knew it was wrong, attacking his cousins without evidence. But he knew the evidence would prove what they all suspected. And Lórcan was right: if Tnúthgal or Ninnid took the throne, their own days might be numbered.

Lórcan shook his head. "I don't know. If the reports we're receiving are correct, we're near even matched by these bandits."

"Their morale and their discipline must be abysmal. If we can get accurate intelligence about their location, bait them onto a field of our own choosing, and not tip them off to our intentions, we may be able to bring them to stand for battle." Eowain was frustrated. Too many times already, the bandits had slipped free when he sought to meet them on their own ground, or had caught his men in ambushes. His success in repulsing their raid at Mynnynrainsh had only made the edge of his frustration sharper.

But Lórcan waved his hand. "Too many risks. They could keep cutting at us like this for weeks, a man here, a man there, and how long before the men lose faith in their crippled king?" Lórcan's voice was bitter and rancorous. "If the men have weeks of this kind of bandit-hunting, it will wear down their own morale and discipline. It will wear away our numbers. It already has."

"We've worn away their numbers as well."

"Aye, some. But they're wearing us worse, I'd wager. If the people lose their faith in us, they'll join up with the bandits rather than replace our own losses." Lórcan shook his head once again. "We can't allow the people to lose their faith in us." He glared at Medyr. "And if we haven't the faith of the drymyn, we won't hold the faith of the people much longer."

Medyr blinked at him. Eowain knew the Lord-Drymyn respected Lórcan, but the Order's regrettable position had been made clear. Medyr didn't answer to any earthly king, but to the Gods and the Mór-Dára.

Lórcan sneered at his drymyn, then turned back to Eowain. "I don't think we have a choice anymore. I have to announce my abdication."

Eowain shook his head. "No, brother. You're my king."

Lórcan spoke through clenched teeth. "No, brother. *You* are *my* king." He turned to the rest of his councilors. "My last order as your king is for you to support my brother and love him better than you have loved me."

They all so swore.

• • •

BITTER WIND SWEPT DOWN the valley of the Gasirad River and rippled the silvered waters under the light of the moon. Eowain puffed at a pipe of linden leaf. Tendrils of smoke curled around his head. He looked out west over Gruiniath. The moon was just past the peak of its fullness, and the night was clear. Snow on the ground gave the night an unreal, blue-silver brilliance.

King. The thought still seemed unreal to him. It was not an office he had sought. Not one he was sure he even wanted. But what were these feelings now within him. Fear? Worry? And maybe even pride? He wasn't sure. Everything seemed a jumble in his heart and his mind.

There across the river was an entire nation of men who wanted nothing more than to see Droma fail. How often in the lives of his father and grandfathers and all the generations of his ancestors had men from those lands challenged their hold on this side of the river? How many lives of Droma had been lost defending it? Droma was the key to the ancient eastern province of Hagall in these parts, the key to a fifth of the High-Kingdom of Iathrann. If Droma fell into chaos, the way would be open for invasion and war. And now it fell to him to defend it.

He looked down at the rough stones of the tower beneath his boots. He took another long, slow draught from the pipe and held the linden smoke a long time before releasing it. He felt its effects creeping over his mind and welcomed the relief. He kicked *at* idly at the tower stones.

Four generations, he thought. Four generations ago, his great-great-grandfather Donnghal had built this tower upon the stony outcropping over the Gasirad's waters. For four genera-tions, the Donnghaile had defended Droma from this point. The

very name of the town and the fort reflected that: *Dúnsciath*. The
Fort of the Shield. It was a great responsibility he held now.

He walked the circumference of the tower. Looking south,
the river widened and split around a long strand in the waters
called the Ailénág, the Island of Battle. And there were the docks
of Dúnsciath's little river port, with barges tied up for the winter
and small, round fishing boats pulled up upon the banks.

Uphill from the waters was the village itself. Smoke rose in
wisps from the thatched round-houses of his people.

And all to the south and the east and the north, everything within a day's ride, it was all his now. His to defend. His
to protect.

Far to the southeast lay his cousin Ninnid's hold-fast. He had
remained quiet through all the tumult, but had done little to stop
the bandits that crossed his borders from Khaibe territory.

And half as far to the north was Crúcavainn, hold-fast
of Tnúthgal.

How am I going to bring an end to this? Eowain kicked again at the
stones of the tower. *Great-great-grandfather, how will I bring peace
to Droma?*

● ● ●

The next morning, before the sun was up, the chamberlain
announced a visitor to the hall of Dúnsciath, seeking audience
with the king. Medyr accompanied Lórcan and Eowain into the
hall. There had been no opportunity yet for the formal rites of
abdication and succession. Despite the intentions of the previous
day's council, Lórcan was still the king.

In the hall waited three figures, hooded and cloaked, attended
by five men of the King's Company watching over them. Each of the
strangers looked the worse for wear, their gear tattered and dirty.

One of Lórcan's soldiers spoke up. "Your Highness. Our
patrol encountered these men on the trail near the thorp
of Gormlyn."

Eowain noticed the soldiers also seemed somewhat worse for wear. "They gave you trouble?"

"No, sir. Archers on the Drægan ridge dropped shafts on us as we returned. We couldn't engage them. We hadn't enough men to spare with these three to watch over."

Eowain gritted his teeth again. Bandit archers in the very heart of the kingdom, not three miles from where they stood. He felt fury growing in his breast.

The soldier went on. "They wouldn't identify themselves, but they presented us with this." He handed over a wooden medallion painted with a lion rampant on a field of green under the red hand of Manech on a field of white. The crest of the Gwynn clan, a token for safe conduct in the lands of the Gwynn's allies. "They insisted on speaking with you, sire."

The strangers wore no other identifying livery. One drew back his hood and bowed to Lórcan. "Your Highness." He was dusky-haired and swarthy.

"For the moment at least." His brother gave Eowain a look and sighed, then turned to the strangers. "Welcome to Dúnsciath. Who are you, then? What's this about?"

The other two strangers drew back their hoods as well. The first man introduced them as his personal guards. "For myself, I am Ciaran son of Turloch of the Gwynn, chief of Dolgallu."

Emissaries from Ardgal of Ivearda? It had been more than a fortnight since their last emissary, the Lady Fidelm, had departed back to King Ardgal's court.

Lórcan and Eowain each bowed an appropriate degree to the man's rank. "Welcome, indeed, Lord Ciaran." Eowain felt something like hope flicker in his heart as his brother went on. "We had the pleasure of your sister's company not a fortnight ago. Is she well?"

Lord Ciaran nodded. "Aye, Your Highness, thank you. She returned to the court of our own king nigh on a week ago with the results of your discussions. I'm sorry to hear about your... condition, Your Highness."

Eowain saw his brother's half-handed fist clench in its

bandages. His brother acted as if he'd heard nothing about his condition. "What news do you bring, Lord Ciaran?"

"Not news, Your Highness, but an entreaty. Our king Ardgal has not yet made his decision, but it is my own daughter who would be the bridegroom to the king of Droma, and I would beg a favor of you."

Lórcan waved Lord Ciaran to a chair at the table, and Eowain instructed the warriors of Droma to take the lord's guards to the kitchen and find food and drink for themselves.

After the guards had left and refreshment had been brought for their guest and the king, the Lord Ciaran continued.

"Your Highness, Lord Eowain, we've heard of the troubles in your kingdom, and I would entreat you to entertain the solution that I offer."

"We'll hear you, sir."

"I appreciate the offer you've made for my daughter's hand. She's a fair, courteous, and gifted woman, and your offer is kind. But our king will not give her and her sixty-two head of cattle away to anyone less than a king."

"And yet you're here? A messenger could have been sent with such unwelcome news."

"I am not here on my king's behalf, Lord Eowain, but on my own. And my daughter's. A drymyn has told me of a curse that will fall on our lands if my daughter doesn't marry into the Clan Donnghaile. But I tell you, I have no liking for this cousin Tnúthgal of yours." Lord Ciaran took a thirsty drink from his cup.

"Then you're in good company, sir. My brother and I like him little ourselves." Lórcan was scowling. "Come now, what would you have us consider?"

"First, you must agree to abide by two conditions."

"You are bold, sir." Lórcan made as if to rise, but Eowain stayed him with a hand on his brother's arm.

Eowain leaned forward. "What're these conditions?"

"My daughter wishes to meet with her intended before any final agreement is struck. And she reserves the right to refuse the match if she finds her bridegroom unworthy."

Medyr nodded. "It is the ancient right of women to agree or not with the choices presented to them for marriage partners. None may gainsay them."

Eowain gestured to the Lord-Drymyn. "We're bound by law to respect your daughter's decision, no matter what else we may agree. You would have our word to honor your second condition."

"You are the Lord Eowain, are you not?" Lord Ciaran eyed him. "I see, lad, that you're handsome, tall, and strong. I've heard tell that you're skilled in arms and mild of temper. In fact, that you're one of the wisest of men — stern to your foes, but a good counsellor on great matters. Is it so?"

Eowain made polite denial, but Lórcan interrupted. "My brother's too humble. He's all of these things and more. A better man than I, in fact. But what of it?"

Lord Ciaran turned now to Lórcan. "Forgive me, Your Highness. But if you will abdicate your crown to your brother, I'm willing to commit thirty men to your cause, in addition to my daughter's birthrights for a dowry."

Shock spread through the room. Bold indeed, as Lórcan had said, for this man to come into a king's hall to ask him to step down from his own throne.

But the shock soon passed. An additional thirty men were sorely needed that day, and might tip the balance of the struggle with Tnúthgal in their favor.

Lórcan seemed grey and grim of a sudden, but said nothing of the previous night's council. He looked instead to his brother, and Eowain nodded in return. "It's decided then." Lórcan rose. "We agree to these terms. I'll announce my abdication this very day."

The three men clasped hands, and Medyr muttered a prayer beneath his breath, asking for the Gods to witness that agreement.

Eowain was still gripping the Lord Ciaran's hand as he asked, "How soon may she be here for us to meet?"

"First, I must tell you news from the trail." They all sat once again at the table and Ciaran leaned in like a conspirator. "In your settlement at Raithneach, we chanced upon a small band of travelers, six men of an unsavory disposition. Though he sought to conceal it, one of them bore a badge, marking him for one of your cousin's men. I overheard them speaking of a gathering at a place called Gruínmór to which they were bound."

Eowain seemed surprised. "The Lady of Gruínmór has ever been our friend, brother."

Lórcan's eyes narrowed as he considered this news. "Why should we believe this is true?"

Lord Ciaran shrugged. "I do not claim that it is, but as I've said, I've no liking for your cousin. If this news aids your cause, then I will be glad to see those brigands destroyed."

Gruínmór lay some six miles to the north, along the High-King's Road. If there were bandits gathering there, a raid might be in the offing. Eowain knew that his Aunt Rathtyen was expecting a caravan of merchants to be passing through Dúnsciath on its way north to Ivea that very day. *Have the bandits learned of it?*

Eowain nodded to Ciaran. "Thank you for this news, lord. We'll consider it well." Lórcan summoned a servant, whispered to him, and sent him away on an errand. "Now, lord," continued Eowain, "when might I meet your daughter?"

To his surprise, Ciaran replied, "As soon as tomorrow if you like, sir. She traveled as far as Trígrianna with me and remained there in disguise while I came to see what manner of man you are for myself." He nodded and laid a finger aside of his nose. "I think now my sister's praise for you was not unwarranted, Lord Eowain. Or should I call you 'king?'"

There was shouting from outside the hall in the courtyard. Medyr went to the door, but it opened from without as he arrived. A guard, breathless, looked at the Lord-Drymyn with surprise, then to the men at the table. "A spy, my lord!"

PART TWELVE

THERE WERE TWO SPIES as it turned out. They had crept
under a shuttered window of the king's hall and eavesdropped on
what was said within. One was captured, but the other escaped.

The captured man's tongue proved stubborn. Despite a vari-
ety of threats, he remained silent. Eowain had other matters to
concern him that day and ordered him to the cellars of the tower
for more exalted forms of persuasion.

•　•　•

THERE WAS NO TIME that day to prepare for the pageantry and
celebration of a formal coronation. That would have to wait until
all the chief-holders of the land could be summoned to witness
the event. But the villagers of Dúnsciath were summoned to the
Hill of Echraide, where the shynn-mound and the barrows of the
kings sat.

Before all assembled, King Lórcan announced his abdication
and revealed the wound that had brought him to that place in
that time.

Then, upon that height, Eowain took his place upon the Stone
of Droma. He knelt before the Lord-Drymyn. Lustral water
spilled cold through his hair and dripped through his beard as
the Lord-Drymyn anointed him. His teeth chattered as the waters
froze upon his cheeks.

"Thára blétsunga, Gydenna Droma, Echraide Egesunga!" The Lord-Drymyn's tremolo voice intoned the ancient rite of the blessing as he laid both hands on the crown of Eowain's bowed head.

Then came the oaths. "Will you solemnly promise and swear to govern the Men of Droma according to their laws and customs? Will you to your power cause Law and Justice, in Mercy, to be executed in all your judgements? Will you to the utmost of your power maintain the Laws of the Gods and the Shynn?"

It seemed his heart was in his throat, but Eowain choked out his vows. "I solemnly promise so to do."

"Will you maintain and preserve inviolably the settlement of the Circle of Droma, and the doctrine, worship, discipline, and government thereof, as by law established in Droma? And will you preserve unto the Drymyn and Brothers of Droma, and to the Groves and Sanctuaries there committed to their charge, all such rights and privileges, as by law do or shall appertain to them or any of them?"

"I solemnly promise so to do."

• • •

IN THE HOURS BEFORE DAWN, Medyr was summoned to attend to the poor wretch of a spy in the tower cellars. He was naked, battered, and bruised. His skin was lacerated as if by small knives and whips. Whatever he might have thought of the prisoner's condition, he kept it to himself. He whispered prayers to alleviate the man's pain and his fear and ministered to his wounds.

Nearby, Lórcan and Eowain were in close conversation.

"He says his chief suspected there might be a secret delegation from the Gwynn here in Droma." Eowain, bare-chested, washed blood from his forearms and hands. The stubbornness of the man's tongue had resisted the blandishments of his interrogators all day, but Eowain had at last taken a personal hand in his questioning.

Lórcan scowled. "And his mate? The spy that escaped?"

"They were supposed to rendezvous with their chief in the wild lands northeast of Monóc Hill."

Lórcan cursed. "We have to assume they heard that Ciaran's daughter is at Trígrianna."

"I'll call our patrols in from the field to rendezvous with us at Trígrianna."

"How many men will you take?"

"Everyone we can spare. Ciaran's daughter is too valuable to them. They'll know they can ransom her to us or to the Gwynn. And if she dies, the Gwynn will never forgive us."

• • •

BEFORE DAWN'S LIGHT had yet broken over the eastern mountains, Eowain led his personal guard and a squad of light archer cavalry in a forced march toward Trígrianna, accompanied by Medyr.

Messengers had been sent across the kingdom and most of the King's Company should have turned toward Trígrianna throughout the night. Lórcan remained at Dúnsciath in command of a mere skeleton garrison.

Medyr rode beside Eowain's chariot as the midday hour approached. It was a cold day, but clear, and the snowfall on the Trígrian trail had been trampled to mud by patrols and travelers.

"Have you ever met Ciaran's daughter, Medyr?"

Medyr nodded his head. "Yes, sire. I was at the court of Ardgal of Ivearda last year. Lord Ciaran and his family were there at that time."

"What's she like?"

"I'd say she was a young woman of exceptional grace, wit, and beauty, Your Highness. She charmed and impressed all who met her."

Eowain shook his head. "But what's she *like*, Medyr?" Since the meeting with Ciaran, it seemed their marriage was going to happen after all. Anxiety roiled in Eowain's gut.

"As I recall, sire, she was skilled in the playing of the lyre. And properly respectful of her parents."

Eowain glared at the Lord-Drymyn and shook his head. "You're not going to tell me anything, are you?"

Medyr shrugged. "She is as she is, Your Highness. It makes little difference. This alliance is valuable to your family and your tribe, whether she's fair or foul."

"What if she doesn't like me?" Eowain remembered the rejection the Lady Aine had handed him as a young man. That humiliation still stung. Would the same thing happen now? And worse, would the whole kingdom, every man, woman, and child of the tribe, know of it? He did not think he could bear that.

"Then you and your brother will be in very dire straits indeed, Your Highness."

They approached what was called the Dúngráig Defile, a steep-sided, narrow gorge where Dúngráig Hill intersected the Drægan Ridge from the north. From atop Dúngráig hill, two mighty shafts rose into the air and flew through the sky like thunder-bolts. One struck the ground, quivering. The other impaled a King's guard through the leg and he screamed.

Then a mighty rock lobbed up into the sky from atop that hill. By then, men were shouting and scrambling for cover. The rock seemed to hang in the sky for a long time. Then it crashed down among Eowain's guard, bounced twice and crushed another man beneath it.

Eowain cried out and his charioteer snapped the reins. The chariot leaped away with the squad of cavalry archers behind him. Medyr spurred his pony after him, and Eowain's guard scrambled on foot to keep up.

Eowain raced through the defile as two more shafts and another stone hurtled from the hilltop down upon his guard. Volley after volley fell, and one of the horsemen went down, then another of the king's guard.

Then Eowain was through the defile, breaking out into the hills north of Drægan Point. The bandits' artillery was behind him. The cavalry archers quickly circled around Eowain and Medyr as he drew up and prepared for an ambush.

But the trail ran on over and through the hills ahead as it always had, past Mynnynrainsh and Raithneach before arriving at Trígrianna. Eowain, with spear and sword in hand, felt his heart thudding against his breast bone, but no further attack came.

The footmen hustled up as well, forming a further hedge around him. Still nothing happened.

Seven men had been injured, but no one had been killed. Medyr dismounted to tend to the wounded, stabilizing them for the rest of the march. Then he was back in the saddle and Eowain called for the men to form up again for the march.

He did not slacken the harsh pace, driving his men to their limit. Still, it was two more hours before they reached the hill of Trígrianna.

The trail wound downhill to a stout stone bridge. The span forded over a deep, swirling stream that ran down in a cascade around a shoulder of the hill from the lake on the other side of the peak.

The grassy hummocks rose in steep slopes from there to the summit some six or seven hundred feet above. The trail up the hillside had been carved into a crease between two steep limestone walls. It was a long mile uphill to a hot meal, and a hard-earned rest.

Snow and rain had left the track wet and muddy. As his troop of men ascended the hill, Eowain heard the clamor of combat. His charioteer snapped at the reins, urging the horses on, and his men spurred themselves to a last effort behind him. *Bless them*, he thought as he crested the shoulder of the hill.

Before him lay at last the village with smoke from its torches and furnaces and hearths rising into the darkening sky. It was not another thousand yards farther down the trail, yet even from there, Eowain could see the burnt out remains of some of its huts.

The last summit of the hill lay off to the south. It stood surmounted by a stout timber watch-tower, set with brands upon its roof and ready to be set a-blaze as a watch fire and a warning to the surrounding settlements. A bell rang from it now, announcing the arrival of Eowain and his men upon the hill.

Trígrianna was not a large village, boasting a mere hundred souls, but it stood in a crucial place upon the borderlands. Somewhat upslope toward the peak was the camp for larger caravans and companies, near where the cattle enclosure stood. Eowain saw cowherds driving the cattle, lowing as they went, into the enclosure for protection. Ten men rigged for combat were preparing to move a spiked timber hedgehog into the gap to close up the cow-pen as best they could.

On the fields outside the village, those elements of the King's Company that had assembled through the night had sallied forth to meet bandits. They were already clashing together, two gangs of men with spears, swords, and arrows, when the bell of the watch-tower rang out. To the rear on each side, horsemen were assembled in reserve.

Eowain put a horn to his lips and blasted a challenge. There was movement then among the horsemen on both sides, but the foot-soldiers were already too concerned with their own lives to notice.

Nigh on twenty horsemen from behind the bandits' line turned to face Eowain and his guard. They formed up for a charge.

Eowain barked orders to his men, then blasted his horn once more. He in his chariot and his own horsemen charged forward as the bandits' cavalry spurred themselves into motion against him. The king's guard ran forward, following their lord. Medyr seized his pony's bridle and led it aside.

From atop a nearby rise, he watched as Eowain's horsemen and a squad of the bandit horsemen traded volleys of bolts, swerving around and across a small hill, trying to flank one another, while another squad of bandit horsemen with spears charged Eowain's chariot and bodyguard. Yet a third squad of heavier horsemen followed behind with swords. With a wild battle cry, Eowain's chariot and his men disappeared into the maelstrom of horses and men.

But from an opposite hill behind their own troops, another squad of brave Droma horsemen charged down from their height, skirted the skirmishing foot-soldiers, and charged down on the melee, adding their strength to Eowain's.

Together, the king's horsemen and guard repulsed the bandits' horsemen. Soon after, their footmen fled as well. Of nigh on three-score men, they left near half wounded or dead upon the field.

Eowain's horsemen harried the fleeing bandits, but Eowain himself rode in his chariot toward the village, leading the infantry in behind him. Medyr soon returned to his side with his pony. When they arrived, Eowain found the chamberlain, the constable of the village, and two guards all sore wounded.

"Damn it!" Eowain cursed as realization dawned on him. The pitched melee outside the village had been only a diversion, and he soon learned the truth of the matter. A smaller force of eight men had fought their way through the village while the rest of the defenders were engaged in the skirmish. They'd wounded these four brave men. And kidnapped the Lady Eithne.

●   ●   ●

MEDYR RETURNED LATE that night to the tower at Dúnsciath, accompanied by a small troop of soldiers, a handful of prisoners, and grim news. Eowain had remained behind to send out heavy patrols into the forested northeastern hills. Medyr suspected he'd chase after the bandits well into the night, yet still not catch them. They'd become adroit at evading his men over the past several weeks.

When Lord Ciaran learned of his daughter's abduction, he set his jaw and nodded. "Then their doom is sealed." Medyr wasn't sure what he meant, but he certainly aimed to bring truth to his words. The drymyn were generally meant to be men of peace and learning, skilled in the arts and sciences. But the skills he'd learned as a healer, a chirurgeon, and an herbalist also gave him vast powers of persuasion. That night, Medyr was not kind. By dawn, the prisoners taken from the field at Trígrianna had revealed their plot. Their chief in the northeast, whether on Tnúthgal's orders or not, wanted the Lady Eithne to wed for himself. He intended to force a ransom for her safety from both her own family and the Donnghaile clan, and maybe claim Droma for himself.

• • •

EOWAIN ARRIVED BACK at Dúnsciath by midday and held private converse with the Lords Ciaran and Lórcan. His patrols and Medyr's interrogations had revealed a number of bandit camps in the hills and marshes to the northeast. He'd sent heavy patrols into those woods to tie down the villains. When he emerged from that meeting, his visage was dark with wrath. "Medyr! You, the village chirurgeon, and your three acolytes are to report to the fort at Ruakhavsa. Now!" He was in no mood to have his will brooked, Medyr could see that.

No more would Medyr ride on his little pony. Instead, he had a light, well-bred war-horse brought forward. It was a whole dappled grey mare, with a handsome white stocking on the right foreleg. She had no unusual markings on her body, but her lips were white, and she bore a white blaze from the fore knot of her mane to the tip of her nose. She'd been a regular patrol horse for some years already, and would be reliable in a short fight.

Or so the king's stable master told him. She was a four-year-old mare with good speed, he said, but had a terrible fear of jumping, which suited Medyr's own courage just fine. He was certainly no horseman.

The quartermaster loaded his horse with grain and provisions. He knew he should not expect to return before the Lady Eithne was rescued. All through the Fort of the Shield, men were making ready for war.

Medyr, his three acolytes, and the village chirurgeon departed within an hour of getting their new king's orders. By nightfall, they arrived at the settlement of Ruakhavsa.

There was a mine there, and a small fort to defend the mining camp. Eowain and his King's Company had taken command of the settlement.

As Medyr and his crew arrived, they met a troop of soldiers returning from the forested hills to the northeast. They looked much the worse for wear. Despite how weary he was from the journey, the men returning from the forests were far worse off. Medyr set up camp with them as they arrived in the village, tending to their wounds. As he worked, he learned they'd been sent into the wild hills between Droma, Ivea, and Cailech, twenty-eight men in all, but had been ambushed by wild crowing bandits of Cailech-men. They'd lost none of their own, but several had been injured in their retreat.

Before night fell, still another patrol returned with a similar tale. They were fortunate to meet their erstwhile ambushers in an open confrontation. They'd skirmished with bows before Eowain's men broke contact and returned to report. Their wounds were few, but their morale was shaken.

Only when there were no further wounded to tend did Medyr leave the chirurgeon and his acolytes to continue setting up a proper hospital. He took himself instead to attend upon his king.

• • •

THE DAYS FOLLOWING became a blur. From his field camp at the mine of Ruakhavsa, Eowain sent patrols into the forests, probing at the bandits, wearing at them.

But they wore at him as well. Ambush and counter-ambush were the order of the day. Beyond the frontier at Ruakhavsa, there was a tall rugged hill that fell down to the east into a long rocky glen, sloping away from Droma into boggy wetlands of pines as it drained the forested hills of rain. At the center of the bog was a hill high enough to be dry and forested. Eowain's spies had the bandits' main camp located on that hill at the center of that bog, some five miles distant. *And that's where I'll find the Lady Eithne.* As long as they held the Lady alive, they had some measure of security there, for Eowain dared not risk an uncertain frontal assault through difficult terrain, lest she be killed before he could reach her.

The bandits had also rigged dead-falls all through the hills leading down to the boggy glen. Their own scouts also not shy to engage, only to pursue. Both sides were husbanded their men and tested one another.

Near the end of the day, with the sun westering in the sky, a messenger riding hard came to Ruakhavsa. He wore the Donnghaile colors and the sigil of the river salmon, but these were surmounted by the crescent of the cadet branch of the clan. Eowain's men ushered him under guard into their king's presence.

He was out of breath and muddy. Whatever news he brought came with urgency. "What is it?" Fear knotted Eowain's guts.

"I bring word, Lord-Captain, from your cousin Tnúthgal."

Eowain felt his chest go tight. Though his coronation had not been formal, it had been ordained, and by now all the kingdom should have known of it. But this man showed him none of the courtesy due to his king.

One of Eowain's men seized him by the scruff of his neck to force him to his knees, but Eowain waved the man off. "What news?"

"He has heard of your campaign against the bandits. Knowing that you have summoned all the King's Company here to deal with these villains, he has raised levies of his own and moved them to defend the Fort of the Shield."

Eowain felt his heart freeze. "He has done what?"

"He wishes me to reassure you that King Lórcan and his guests are well and comfortable within the Tower of Donnghal."

Eowain thanked the messenger for his service and sent him away to find hospitality where he might, then ordered scouts sent out to Dúnsciath. Their reports confirmed the messenger's words. Tnúthgal had taken up positions around the tower and the fort, ostensibly to defend it. But Eowain understood the message his cousin had sent. Dúnsciath, with his brother and the father of his betrothed, were besieged. If Eowain failed to deal with these bandits once and for all, Tnúthgal would starve Lórcan into submission, take the tower, and demand elections. Humiliated by such a turn of events, Eowain would surely be removed from office, and Tnúthgal would become king.

•   •   •

DOWN OFF THE HEIGHTS of the eastern mountains came terrible grey clouds. They descended down the forested hills toward Eowain's camp at Ruakhavsa, driven by the winds, and great white clumps of snow fell from them.

Two days earlier, Eowain had called up the peasant levies from his clients. They'd been trickling in from the countryside for the last few days with little training and the meanest of gear. Eowain began sending them out to bolster his patrols.

From an old ruined settlement where some bandits had camped, Eowain's left flank had been harried by villains while his patrols pressed further and further northeast. He wanted that flank secured. He sent a score of these peasants to seize the old ruin. The peasants fared well and set the bandits to flight.

Meanwhile, a troop of Eowain's men encountered a band of robbers nigh on three score strong foundering in the snow north of Bankern and engaged them, scattering them into the forest and the snowy wilderness.

But as reports of these successes early in the day came back, the snowstorm grew stronger. Eowain gathered Medyr and his officers into the little thatch-and-daub roundhouse that had been commandeered for them. Outside, the wind howled down from the mountains, shrieked like a *ban-shynn* through the trees, and drove heavy, wet snow before it.

"Medyr, you must entreat the Gods. If this storm continues, we'll be penned here in this little fort, and the damned brigands will slip our grasp again."

Medyr looked at him with grave eyes. "The Gods, they are forgetful, Your Highness. Their Powers may be summoned, when used with the proper words and shapes, but there's a cost. The Watcher must be reminded of the Covenant it swore with the Shynn and our Race, else it will turn on us and ravage the land."

Eowain feared more what the bandits might do to his land and what Tnúthgal might do at the tower if the storm fenced him into the fort. "You must do it. We have to end this."

Medyr shook his head. There seemed to be true fear in his eyes, and Eowain wondered if he'd ever seen his mentor so afraid. "The Gods are forgetful and very far away. If the rite is not performed precisely, if it's changed by even one line or dot, by even so much as a hair's breadth, it will be rendered valueless or worse. A broken star is the Gate of Annwn, the Gate of Death." His eyes seemed haunted then by a vision of something no one else could see, and his whisper was full of dread. "The Gate of the Shadows and the Shells."

Eowain had stripped the kingdom to bring the Company of the Shield here. He'd left a mere skeleton crew as garrison in Dúnsciath. How many men would die if these bandits were allowed to escape now? What would happen at Dúnsciath if Tnúthgal, seeing Eowain trapped here, turned his own levies against the king's seat? Lórcan would be killed, he was sure, and the Lady Eithne's father beside him. "Then recite your incantations as they are written. Prepare your rituals without erring. In the proper places and times render your sacrifices. Whatever's necessary, Lord-Drymyn. Whatever the price."

PART THIRTEEN

With great reluctance, Medyr finally agreed. Eowain didn't understand what it might cost him, didn't realize how steep the price really was. Magick was not a thing in which one meddled like a child in a mud-hole.

Fearful that any error might cost the kingdom more gravely than any imagined, he sent away Eowain and all his men. Only his own three acolytes remained, his young students in the ways of the Order.

He ordered the fire stoked hot and he carved the *coelbreni* runes in the dirt floor at precise locations. He mixed potions, infusions, incenses, and elixirs, until all present were dizzy with smoke, *uisce*, and perfumes. Then he began to chant in that most ancient tongue.

"Windrægast, myndgath!"

Medyr's acolytes joined their master in his chanting. He'd been teaching them this tongue, for it was the ancient tongue of Men from the days before the Great Settlement, the language of magick taught to Men by the Shynn long ago. Their tongues were yet rough, but they followed the patterns he established.

Before long, there arose about him, glowing to his eyes, a whirlwind of threads arising up out of the dust of the humble little hovel. He felt the earth beneath his seat, felt its age and its timeless strength rising up through him.

Medyr redoubled their chanting. The acolytes began drum-
ming. The relentless rhythms became chaotic, directed by Medyr's
chants, and power rose up through him, swirling up into a dome
to the roof of that little round house.

Windrægast, myndgath!

For thirteen hours, they chanted. The acolytes swayed at their
places, near to exhaustion, but Medyr urged them on. There
could be no wavering, no errors, lest their will be found insuffi-
cient to the task.

Windrægast, myndgath!

Without the thorp, the howling winds tapered and came less
shrill through the barren trees. The heavy snow fall slackened.
Thick fog settled upon Ruakhavsa. A man couldn't see as far as
fifty yards in that murk. It thickened through the day, batting the
countryside like clumps of new-shorn wool, until a man had to
struggle to see even a dozen yards.

Later, Medyr would learn that on all the rest of the hills of
Droma and Ivea and Cailech thereabouts, snow fell as deep as a
tall man's knee.

But in the four settlements around Ruakhavsa and up into the
hills, that heavy fog writhed between the trees like a cat scratching
its back upon the dead and brittle branches.

And there in the shadows of the hut? What rough beast
slouched forth that night into the world?

• • •

SCOUTS REPORTED FOG as far as a mile and a half north of
the little hut where Medyr and his acolytes mumbled. Eowain took
advantage of it. He moved troops up to the crest of the hill overlooking Ruakhavsa. They skirmished with targets of opportunity
and dug into new positions.

Late in the night, Eowain called Medyr to the headman's
roundhouse where he'd taken residence.

He looked up from a parchment scroll with charcoal signs and symbols scraped onto it as Medyr entered. "That fog?"

The Lord-Drymyn seemed weary and old, his eyes dark and haunted. He shrugged, and his voice was the barest whisper. "Sometimes, the Gods remember."

Eowain nodded. "I like them when they do that." He waved Medyr to the table. As the drymyn came around to view it, Eowain presented to him a map of the lands around Ruakhavsa. There were many marks and symbols on the hills to the north, and again near the bog to the northeast. Another sign showed the bandit chief's hill in the center of that mire.

Eowain pointed to the marks on the northern hill. "We've got two troops up there with a squad of light cavalry archers, strung out over a mile across the crest of the hill. I've got another troop of infantry and a squad of medium cavalry across a line north of Bankern."

Medyr nodded. "Yes, I see. You intend to screen your footmen's advance down the glen with your cavalry archers on the hill top, then advance with medium horse and foot straight down the fold of the land."

"Exactly." Eowain pointed to another part of the map. "The problem is here." With first and third finger forked, he indicated two positions on the map near the western edge of the bog, about a mile and a half from the cottage in which they stood. "Beyond here, there's half a foot of snow on the ground. There are fording points here and here, but they're marshy bottlenecks, and one of them leads straight into a steep, uphill battle on the other side."

Medyr stroked at his chin. "The snow is going to slow your men down. And you can't charge through that bog with horses, which means your footmen will be in the lead, taking withering fire from their archers and spearmen as you cross."

"Exactly. If they have as many men as reports indicate—."

Medyr raised a finger. "Which is how many, Your Highness?"

"Maybe a hundred, half of them a rabble with archers for support, the rest mounted. They won't charge us across the bog, but they can contain any breakout."

"So the problem is to get across these fords to the top of this hill? Against nigh on fifty men with spears, swords, and bows at each crossing point? With what, three troops a-foot?"

"Aye. About ninety men."

Medyr whistled and shook his head. "A hard fight."

"And all they have to do is fall back with the Lady Eithne, deeper into Cailech territory. For all we know, they might have done so already."

"There is another way." Medyr pointed to the map, south of the glen. "A team of men could follow the crest of this hill down to the confluence of the glen, crossing here, and take them from behind."

●　●　●

THE NEXT MORNING, a troop of bandits tested Eowain's strength on the hill above Ruakhavsa, and his archers dissuaded them from attempting an assault uphill against them. Meanwhile, Eowain's scouts patrolled the route Medyr had outlined on the map.

They returned to report finding a crew of bandits with a siege crossbow in some old ruins on the crest of the hill. The scouts had taken the nest from them. They'd also run down a patrol from the bandit's stronghold. In both cases, they'd let no word of their mission escape back to the bandit chief. They'd disabled traps where they'd found them, and the way seemed clear for Eowain's purpose.

●　●　●

THE NEXT MORNING, Eowain set off in secret to the northeast with Medyr, his personal guard and a troop of ten foot-men. By midday, they crested the hill north of Trigrianna, where he found the siege crossbow his patrol had secured and left behind. He took that for a sign that the bandits weren't yet aware that this outpost on their flank had been compromised.

He had a crew quick and quiet pack it up to take with them, then turned northward. He could hear shouts and clashes from across the glen, where the elements of the King's Company on the opposite hill crest had sortied against the bandits as a diversion.

Damn! They were early. He wouldn't have much time now. He and his men had to get to the bandit camp before the daylight waned if they were going to have any chance. The villain's lair was only two miles from his position as the ravens flew, but he'd have to lead his men twice that distance around as much of the snowy marshlands as they could avoid. Elsewise, they'd be bogged down as they assaulted up-hill.

The hills were thickly forested there, the trees bare. The storm had torn down the last frozen green summer leaves that still clung to branches. They littered the snow like glittering emeralds cast off by a careless child.

He found a low narrow place about two miles east-northeast of the ruins and crossed it with his men. A quick, quiet climb on the other side put them atop a small rise due east from the bandits. Behind him, mighty Ydrys loomed some sixty miles distant under white-shrouded slopes. The going was hard in the snow, more so with the need to stay silent. The chief of these villains was no fool, he'd proven that. He wouldn't leave his back unguarded.

There was another low narrow place then. A trickle of icy water ran through it, and the ground all about was sodden. Eowain's boot squelched through muck up to his ankles, and his men and his drymyn churned the snow brown behind them.

Eowain took the van himself. He had to prove his courage, no matter how concerned Medyr and his guard were for the safety of their new king. He had to show his mettle here, or lose their faith before he'd fully earned it. The turn in the weather had been fortunate, or so it had seemed. But he feared that boon might turn dark and ominous. *The Gods, after all, are forgetful.*

He heard a branch snap ahead of him, and a careless whistle of relief. With the spear of his father in his strong right hand and his sword in the other, he pounced.

The single man on guard had grown careless. He'd been stomping around in a vain effort to warm himself. Eowain's sword point went through his throat like a hungry man through pudding. For a long moment, he stared wide-eyed at his killer. Eowain gritted his teeth and gave the blade a final push, splitting the bones at the back of the man's neck.

Across the hill, the wild melee of his diversion had drawn the strength of these villains to the west. Nothing more stood in his path.

Eowain and his troop howled up the bandit's hill from the east like a sleuth of angry bears, striking at their rear. He had them outnumbered in the camp nigh on two to one, but he didn't linger for a slaughter. He had but one mission: find and rescue the Lady Eithne. His troop skirmished with the enemy while he and Medyr ransacked their way through the camp.

He found her where he expected, in the only large and well-kept pavilion on the hill. She proved to be a petite, fair-skinned, red-headed waif of a girl, bound and gagged, but the look she gave him as he cut his way in past the guards froze him where he stood, more surely than any winter storm. Her green eyes glittered like the frozen summer leaves, but not with fear. The ferocious anger he saw there should have struck him dead upon the spot.

A hoarse shout from without told him that their time was over. The bandit chief knew by now he'd been duped and his prize was in jeopardy. He'd be returning with as much fury as he could muster to defend it.

Eowain sheathed his bloody sword and hauled her ungraciously to her feet. Without a word, he hefted her up onto his shoulder.

• • •

EOWAIN BOUNDED FROM the chieftain's tent as she kicked and squirmed. His bodyguard contested with the bandit-chief and his men, but upon seeing their king with his prize, they broke off and away they all went, fleeing headlong through the bracken, deep snow and marshy ford, ice crackling beneath their boots.

As the bandits pursued them into the ford, a squad of Eowain's archers let loose their clothyard shafts and discouraged them from close pursuit. The howl of the bandit chief echoed through the glen.

As he and his men fled back toward his own lands as fast as their legs would carry them, Eowain blew three strident blasts upon his horn.

The bandit pursuit soon fell away and Eowain slackened his pace. The woman struggled on his shoulder. She was going to knock him over in the snow if she persisted, so he granted her liberty.

The Lady Eithne's visage was stern and wrathful. She spoke not a word, despite being unbound. She spoke not a word, though Eowain announced himself king of Droma and friend to her father. She spoke not a word no matter how he entreated her to do so. She insisted instead, and by indignant gestures alone, on a stout pair of boots. She refused to go one step farther until she had them and stomped away once she did, southwest toward Bankern as Eowain indicated.

She spoke not a word throughout their flight from the bandit camp, nor would she let anyone touch her or offer her anything for food or water, not even Medyr.

Eowain could only imagine how angry she was, how fearful the whole abduction had been for her. And gods only knew what those villains had done while they had her. He gave her as wide a berth as seemed prudent, but he worried that being carried off like a sack of potatoes by yet another strange and warlike man had not done much to earn him respect in her eyes. Her silence was a palpable thing, and it was well after midnight before he could lead them back to Bankern.

There, Eowain heard the reports of his troop leaders. On the signal of his three blasts, his men had fallen back from the hilltop to the security of the small fort at Ruakhavsa, where they'd fortified the thorp.

Bankern by comparison offered little in the way of defense. It was un-walled and its people had fled for fear of the fighting. Eowain had no choice but to lead them on to the greater security of Ruakhavsa.

They arrived there in the dark well after middle-night amid a welter of confusion. A bleating, crying, shoving mass of livestock, women, and children had come from the countryside all about for protection. His men were driving them into the ring-fort. Palisade hurdles around the base of the hill and the strong gate house were well-lit with torches. Soldiers cried the watch.

Eowain was weary and grim as he marched into Ruakhavsa, but pleased as well to see the preparations. "Now we'll see what stones those bastards have," he said to Medyr. He gave over the care of the Lady Eithne, who had still spoken not a word, to his drymyn.

He didn't know what to make of that silence, and made the rounds of the defenses, to inspect his engineers' improvements. Shouting orders, he commanded a *recon* patrol up into the glen to assess the bandits' movements.

Medyr ushered the Lady into the chieftain's roundhouse, for-tified with stones and mortar, where she was given maids to attend to her and the dubious safety of the chief-holder's cellars.

A few men had been wounded in the diversionary attacks, and Medyr soon attended to them. He was still at his work when the dawn arose over the mountains.

•   •   •

THE PATROL EOWAIN had sent into the hills had been gone for hours already. It was six miles to the confluence of the glen and the bandit camp. They hadn't been heard from since they'd left. Once the last bandages were applied, Medyr joined the rest of the camp in watching and waiting for them with apprehension. The sun continued to rise into toward the midday sky, and still no word came.

Eowain returned to the chieftain's round-house. "The Lady?"

"Safe in the cellars below, with maids to attend her and stout men at the door." Medyr was sitting on a bench in the chieftain's house. He looked to Eowain like he hadn't slept in days.

"Good. Tnúthgal will have had time to hear of this setback from the leader of these robbers. The full-strength of the bandits may be upon us soon. We should beware Tnúthgal's strength to our west." Eowain felt sudden weariness creep over him. He hadn't slept in days himself, but he hoped it didn't show. He had to give his men and his kingdom no reason to doubt him.

Medyr handed him a cup of tea and guided him to a seat on the bench. "Here, sit down a while, Your Highness. You have been stalwart, but you must rest now. Your men will be looking to you when the time comes."

Eowain sat and sipped at the tea. "If Tnúthgal should rise with his clients against me and join the bandits, we may not be able to hold this position for long."

"Then we can't let that happen, Your Highness. Tnúthgal is overbold if he trusts these bandits to his cause now, I think."

Eowain seemed doubtful. "After that storm? This bandit chief's men will be desperate for food and plunder? I'm not sure my cousin's trust would be so ill-placed."

"Aye, but bandits don't stand and fight. They pick and parry. If Tnúthgal orders them to an assault, we have only to hold them until their courage folds. If Tnúthgal doesn't reinforce them from his levies, that won't take long."

"I hope you're right."

Medyr's tone became grave. "Your Highness?" Eowain looked up at him. "I find your lack of faith disturbing." Medyr smiled and patted his shoulder.

Eowain shook his head. "You're the one always telling me the Gods are forgetful."

Shouts arose from the gate house and the towers. Eowain leaped to this feet and rushed out to the nearest tower. His cup of tea lay forgotten upon the floor. Leaping the rungs of a ladder three at a time, he looked out to over the palisade and the fields beyond.

The patrol was returning. They ran from the forest as if all the hounds of Annwn were upon their heels. The men in the gatehouse and the towers cheered at the sight of them.

Then came the angry mob of bandits at their rear.

"To arms!" The cry rang out from every throat. The fort bristled with activity. Men took up spears, bows, swords, hammers, and any other weapon at hand. Medyr joined Eowain upon the tower, overlooking the margin of the fort. The patrol, a mere handful of men on light mounts, were riding hard. Bandits on light mounts pursued them, heavier horsemen followed, and a rabble on foot boiled from the wood with a roar.

Eowain raised a hand and a hush fell among the good men of Droma. He stood upon the tower, a wind from the northwest riffling his fox-fur cloak, the spearhead of his father Findtan raised to the sky. He watched.

No.

He waited.

Not yet.

He held up the spear of his father yet higher.

Now.

He lowered the spearhead at the gathering gang of villains.

From the fort, the engines thumped as three catapults and two heavy crossbows sent missiles over the heads of his patrolmen and down into the mass of charging horsemen in pursuit.

Eowain did not wait to see the result. He leaped from the watchtower to his chariot. Down in the courtyard of the fort, the patrol raced in through the opening gates. Eowain blasted thrice upon his mighty horn and called the men of Droma to war. His charioteer snapped the reins, and Eowain sallied through the gate and out upon the field of battle.

With a wild cry, his bodyguard and cavalry thundered out from the fort with some four-score men of foot behind them, howling to the fray. Glinting in the cold, midday sun of winter, steel flashed and blood sprayed. Eowain rode his chariot into the melee, feeling for a moment like a hero of old. Feeling for a moment as he imagined his father had often felt.

Then he hacked and slashed and stabbed, leaped to the yoke-pole and thence into the mob.

•   •   •

THE BATTLE WENT ON for some time and the sun was sinking when messengers came on fast horses from the west. They flew Eowain's banners and Medyr received them on behalf of his new king. Lord Tnúthgal, the king's cousin and rival, had raised his levies from their position at Dúnsciath. He had returned without violence north into his own lands. The bandits would get no relief.

At last, the ruffians broke and fled the field. Eowain blasted the pursuit upon his horn and followed them into the forested hills.

•   •   •

THE SUN WAS SETTING when at last he returned to Ruakhavsa. He was slumped in his chariot, driving himself as he rode into the small fort. His charioteer, brave man that he was, had taken a spear and died in his king's arms. Eowain had wrapped the body in his own cloak. It rode in honor with him in his chariot.

Thunderous cheers greeted him as he and his men came to rest in the courtyard.

Eowain stepped down into Medyr's waiting hands, wearied to the bone. "If so many as half a dozen of them escaped, I'd be surprised. One of their retreating elements rallied and ambushed the troop pursuing them, but our men cut them down. The rest of them bogged down where the snow begins, and that's where we finished them."

"Wounded? Killed?" Medyr's voice was concerned.

"Of men of note? My charioteer and two men of my guard are killed. Of the rest, perhaps a dozen dead, and many more injured. Few escaped the day unscathed, I think."

Eowain was pleased to be one of them. Though his kit was splattered with the blood and mud of the field, by luck or courage he'd broken the bandit gang's strength yet taken no wound himself. But he knew his grim news of the field would mean many long hours of chirurgery for Medyr and his acolytes, and grief for families across the kingdom.

As he stood there, a patrol arrived from Dúnsciath. The Lord Ciaran of the Gwynn rode with them, and Eowain greeted him with the good news. Together, he escorted the relieved father to the cellar doors, still shuttered from within and guarded by two stout men.

The doors were cast open. It was a rough, unfinished hole beneath the fort, crowded with the sheep and pigs and women and children both high- and low-born. There among them all stood the Lady Eithne of Dolgallu, like a diamond amid so many coins.

She raised her chin in the torchlight and her fierce green eyes flashed. With calm grace, she stepped up from the cellar. Her father took her by the shoulders and held her before him. His eyes glimmered with torchlight and tears.

At last, the Lady Eithne spoke. "I'm unharmed, Father. The bandit-chief treated me with the dignity due to a lady of rank. And King Eowain and his men have been thus far too preoccupied with their little war to have troubled me."

Eowain stammered. "My lady—."

She turned to look at him. Her face was stern.

King Eowain of Droma knelt in the dirt at her feet. "My lady.

I am ashamed to have permitted your abduction by these robbers and for the indignities you have been forced to suffer. I am humbled to report to you that their strength has been broken. The bandit scourge plaguing Droma is ended, and half-a-hundred villains now pay the Great Queen's price to the soil of this land."

The lady seemed relieved and her stern expression softened. "And the bandit chief?"

Eowain shook his head. "Escaped, I am sorry to say, with a small band of loyal men."

The lady's expression grew troubled. "Then I fear to say that your troubles here in Droma may not yet be at an end."

Eowain rose from his knee, and there was a tense and expectant pause. *Will she forgive me for her abduction? Will she find me a pleasing choice for husband? Will there be peace between Droma and Ivearda at last?* He hadn't felt as anxious in the midst of battle as he felt at that moment, but he ventured into that silence. "We are pleased to welcome you at last to Droma, Lady."

Her calm, cool expression turned to reserved relief, and she permitted herself a slight smile and bowed to the appropriate degree. "I am honored to meet you, Your Highness. And grateful to you for relieving me from the distress of the bandit company." She rose. "But I hope this is not the limit of your hospitality. I could use a hot fire, a more suitable change of clothes, and, if it's not too much to ask, perhaps a hot meal and some honeyed tea?"

Relief swept through him, and Eowain couldn't resist a grin. So it seemed he was at least forgiven. By dint of his bravery and courage, he'd rescued the lady and secured the kingdom for himself and his family. The rest was yet to be seen, but for that day, he had won enough victories.

Here ends
The Hedge King in Winter,
first tale in the Matter of Manred.

ABOUT THE AUTHOR

MICHAEL E. DELLERT lives in the Greater New York City area. Following a traditional publishing career spanning nearly two decades, he now works as a freelance writer, editor, publishing consultant, and writing coach. He is also the sole writer, editor, and publisher of the blog *MDellertDotCom: Adventures in Indie Publishing*. He holds a Master's Degree in English Language & Literature from Drew University, and a certificate from the Cornell University School of Criticism & Theory (2009). *Hedge King in Winter* is his first published fiction novella.

FORTHCOMING WORKS

in the

MATTER OF MANRED SAGA

A Merchant's Tale

The Romance of Eowain

The Wedding of Eithne

Heron's Cry

Join the mailing list at mdellert.com/blog/mailing-list/ to receive more information, news, updates, and special promotional offers on these and other exciting new titles coming soon from Skylander Press.

Made in the USA
Middletown, DE
01 March 2016